The Adventures
of
Jimmy
SCAR
433950
Sch
D0179008

JEANNE
WILLIS

Andersen Press • London

First published in 2001 by
Andersen Press Limited,
20 Vauxhall Bridge Road, London SW1V 2SA

This edition first published in 2003

British Library Cataloguing in Publication Data available
ISBN 1 84270 230 0

Typeset by FiSH Books, London WC1
Printed and bound in Great Britain by Mackays of Chatham Ltd,
Chatham, Kent

For K. Willis

Chapter 1

Gemma tried not to yell, but the hairbrush was completely tangled in her thick, brown curls and instead of rolling it the right way, her father was twisting it tighter and tighter until the hairs at the nape of her neck were ready to snap.

'Ouch!'

He let go of the brush handle as if it had suddenly become red hot.

'Sorry, I'm sorry.'

He slumped down by the window and put his head in his hands. 'It's useless,' he sighed. 'What are we going to do?'

At first, she thought he was talking about her plaits. Ever since she was three, he'd insisted on putting her hair into plaits because that's what her mother had done. Even so, he dreaded doing it, because he was no good at it.

He was a builder and while he was completely at ease with bricks and the cold, hard tools of his trade, girls' hair was a very different matter. It was soft and alive. He was afraid to touch it and that made him clumsy.

'Dad, why don't I just cut it all off?' said Gemma. She'd managed to untangle the brush and was putting her school tie on now.

'Sorry, what?'

'If I had my hair cut, it would save a lot of messing about.'

He picked up an opened letter from the kitchen table and sighed. 'Right now, I'm more bothered about this.'

Gemma recognised the writing paper immediately. It was from Mr Kasheffi.

'Not another one,' she said. 'Why does he want us out of this flat so desperately? We haven't done anything wrong, have we, Dad?'

He looked hurt.

'Fallen behind with the rent, do you mean?'

'No, I know you'd never...'

She trailed off. The last firm he'd worked for still hadn't paid him after his van was trashed and he'd had three bills in a row. Gas, electricity and water.

'We'll get round it,' he said. 'I've got a new job coming up, haven't I? There's a drive wants laying on one of the big houses in Skyswood Road. And they want a garden wall building.'

He seemed to cheer up a bit.

'Can I help in the summer holidays? *Please*, Dad!' Gemma jigged up and down. 'I could help you mix the concrete and...'

'Hey... a building site's no place for you,' he laughed. 'You'll get filthy.'

'So?'

Gemma brushed her hair forward, hiding the thin scar that ran from the bottom of her ear to the corner of her right eye.

'No, it's too dangerous, Gem.'

She wanted to shout, 'Stop saying that, I'm not made of china!' but she didn't dare. If she tried to do anything the slightest bit dangerous, she was afraid the stress might kill him.

'I'd be very careful, Dad.'

'Your mum was careful,' he snapped. 'It didn't save her though, did it?'

They never caught the driver who'd swerved onto the pavement and smashed into Gemma's mother while she was pushing the pram. Gemma couldn't remember much about the accident. She had a fuzzy dream sometimes, about falling through the air and sirens and screams but that was all. Apart from the scar, of course. That hadn't faded.

Every time her hair was pulled back into plaits, there it was for all to see. A constant reminder to her father that she was almost killed and could be again and a good enough reason for the other kids to call her names.

She grabbed her packed lunch. It wasn't much. The only thing she could find in the cupboard was a small packet of cereal, a little pot of fruit in jelly and four tins of dog food.

They hadn't got a dog. Mr Kasheffi wouldn't allow tenants to keep animals in the flats, but she always left food out for the strays in the morning and again when she got home.

'I'd rather be on a building site than at school,' she mumbled, rattling in the drawer for the old tin opener. Her father looked over the top of the letter he was re-reading.

'Don't say that, Gem. Don't be like me.'

Why not? She loved the way he could take a plank of wood and turn it into something completely different. It was magical, this conjuring up of things from nothing. She'd sit and watch, mesmerised, as his hammer rose and fell so easily, it seemed like part of his arm.

'What's wrong with being like you, Dad?'

He started clearing the breakfast things.

'I'm thick, me. If I'd stayed on at school instead of brickying for my dad, we wouldn't be here now, would we?'

'I like it here,' she insisted.

'This grotty dump?' He rolled his eyes. 'You're joking, aren't you?'

It was a late Victorian building divided into flats. They lived on the ground floor, over the basement. True, it was a bit damp and the windows rattled, but the ceilings were high and what was left of the moulding looked like icing on a wedding cake.

There was a large, overgrown garden out the back. It was meant to be shared, but Mr Southam was the only one who did any gardening and he left two years ago. Mr Kasheffi persuaded him to go, even though he'd been living in the top flat quite happily for forty years. After he left, the roses threw out great arches of thorny shoots and refused to bloom.

Gemma never had the chance to say goodbye to Mr Southam. She used to go and knock on his door every Saturday because he gave her extra tins to feed the dogs, but the last time she'd visited, his flat door had been torn off its hinges and all the floorboards had been ripped up. There was no sign of him.

The same thing had happened on the first floor. A Spanish student lived there once. He never spoke to anyone and Gemma never saw him because he always left very early and came home when she was in bed. He never went into the garden. The only reason she knew he'd existed at all was because he sometimes played a guitar.

By the sound of his music, she imagined he must be lonely.

No one had ever lived in the basement as far as she knew.

Gemma attacked the can of dog food with the tin opener.

'Mind yourself. You'll have your thumb off!'

'Dad. I'm all right, honest!'

'Come here, I'll do it.'

He took the can from her, opened it swiftly and dumped the contents into a small plastic bowl. She wanted to beat him on the chest with her fist. 'I could have done that! Why won't you let me!' But she didn't. She just took a deep breath and counted silently to ten.

'Make sure you come home on the bus with Ziggy, won't you?'

'I always do.'

Ziggy was seventeen, and German. She was an au pair, responsible for taking one of the infants home who had a sister in Gemma's class. Gemma's father had arranged for Ziggy to escort Gemma home too, with the infant. Embarrassing in the extreme, because the older sister was allowed to walk home with her friends.

'Got your key, Gem?'

It was round her neck on a string. She showed him. He gave her a kiss.

'So, straight home and if anyone knocks, don't let them in and if anyone rings, don't say I'm not in. I'll be a bit late tonight. Got to see when Mrs Ellis wants me to start that drive, okay?'

She stood there with the bowl of dog food, waiting for him to end his list of dos and don'ts.

'And don't touch the cooker.'

'I won't.'

She picked up her school bag as he held the front door open for her.

'Mind yourself by the dustbins. There might be glass.'

She pulled a face, but he couldn't see. She had her back to him. She held her hand up, waving her fingers without turning, waiting for the door to shut.

Clunk... but he'd be watching her from the window until she was safely on the bus. Always half-smiling, half-believing he'd never see her again.

''Bye, Gem.'

She put the dog food down by the bins. Wolfie was already there, waiting for her. He had a small, nervous terrier with him. It kept jumping forward towards Gemma and then backwards, as if it was on a spring.

'It's all right, Mr Ping, I'm going,' she said. 'Leave him some, Wolfie.'

Gemma patted the massive dog's scabby neck and ran to catch the bus.

Some of the girls were crying in the bus on the way home. It was the last day of term. After the holidays, they would be off to their new schools. Best friends would be split up. Friends who had known each other since they were four.

Gemma sat quietly, squashed against the window next to Ziggy, who had the infant on her lap. Ziggy nudged her.

'Be you next year Gemma, yes? Last day at Junior school! But why are they crying?'

She pulled a face.

'I would laugh!' she said. 'Ha, ha! Like that. It's nicer to be grown-up, I think.'

Gemma smiled automatically, only half-listening. Ziggy watched her for a moment.

'You look very different without plaits,' she said. 'I can't see what you are thinking, hiding behind all that hair.' She parted one side of Gemma's hair back.

'Hello, in there,' she said. 'Anyone at home?'

Gemma put her hand up to cover her scar.

'Don't hide it!' said Ziggy. 'I *love* that scar. How did you get it?'

'A car ran into my pram when I was little.'

'No, really?' Ziggy raised her eyebrows and looked impressed. 'Wow! Did it hurt?'

Gemma shook her head. 'No...I don't know. All I can remember is what Dad's told me. He reckons I nearly died. That's why he won't let me walk home from school. He won't let me do anything!'

Gemma hadn't realised quite how angry she was. The other girls weren't ashamed to cry and suddenly it seemed the right moment to pour her heart out to Ziggy, right there on the bus.

Ziggy sat and listened, unblinking. When Gemma had finished, she pushed her fingers through her thick, short hair and pretended to pull it out.

'Agggggh! How can you stand it? I would walk out.'

She unbuttoned the cuff on her thin blouse and showed Gemma her upturned wrist. It was criss-crossed with little raised, white scars.

'Look. I did that when I went mad,' she smiled. 'I love to look at them. They remind me I am out of prison.'

'Prison?' Gemma gasped. 'You were in *prison*?'

Ziggy took a cigarette out of her handbag and lit it.

'I was in my father's house,' she said. 'Same thing.'

Gemma watched the smoke rise from the cigarette. Any minute now, the driver would stop the bus and tell her to get rid of it. No smoking allowed. Smoking was dangerous and stupid, but for a minute, Gemma wanted to be Ziggy, blowing smoke and not caring.

'Of all the places in the world, why did you come to *England*, Ziggy?' she asked. 'It's not safe and it's not exactly beautiful, is it?'

The bus pulled up at a stop outside a row of small, tatty-looking shops. An old man wrapped in a filthy old curtain spat on the pavement and swore loudly at the sky. Ziggy tapped on the window and blew him a kiss. Gemma was mortified.

'Ziggy, don't!'

'Oh, come on. To be safe and beautiful is pretty boring, don't you think?'

The bus driver was coming over. He was about to tell Ziggy to put her cigarette out, but she ground it under her heel before he could complain.

'Can't you read? ' he said, pointing to the no smoking signs. Ziggy opened her eyes wide.

'*Ich kann Sie nicht verstehen*,' she said.

The driver looked at her suspiciously, tapped his nose and strode back to his seat.

'Fah! Flippin' foreigners.'

To be safe and beautiful was very boring. Gemma looked at her refection in the window. 'Do you think I'd look all right with my hair short?' she said.

Ziggy twisted Gemma's hair back in one hand and considered her from every angle.

'Ja. It would look...cool,' she said. 'I'll cut it for you if you want.'

So, it was agreed that as her father would be home late, Ziggy would go back to Gemma's and crop her hair into a boyish style that wouldn't even need combing to look good.

Gemma let Ziggy into the flat, turned the television on to amuse the infant and fetched the kitchen scissors.

'Go on then,' she said.

Ziggy guided her towards the dressing-table mirror, pushed her down onto the stool by the shoulders and tucked a towel around her.

'Are you brave?' she said.

Gemma nodded and closed her eyes. She felt Ziggy run the comb through the length of her hair, smoothing it down with her palm against her back.

There was a short pause. Gemma felt as if she was about to be executed. There was a small tug as the scissors bit into her hair. She heard the hair plop onto the lino. Then the cold blades slid round her ears, along her neck, over her skull. The back of her head felt strangely exposed and she shivered. Ziggy whisked the towel away.

'You can look now,' she said.

Gemma blinked. She barely recognised the girl in the mirror. At first she was shocked. Then she felt a broad, uncontrollable grin stretching her lips wider and wider, showing her teeth.

'I like it,' she beamed.

'*Das ist gut*. You look fantastic,' said Ziggy.

Ziggy picked up the long strands of fallen hair and plaited them into a fat braid. She held it up. 'Want to keep it?'

Gemma wrinkled her nose.

'Nah. Chuck it in the dustbin outside.'

After Ziggy had gone, she swept up all the little snips of hair and shook them out of the window. There was a dog standing outside, staring back at her. She'd never seen it before. It was a Saluki with long, pale fur. It would have been elegant except that its belly was slung very low, as if it were full of puppies.

Gemma leant out of the window and called to her. 'Here, girl!'

The dog started to walk over cautiously, but then Wolfie galloped into view and she turned and waddled off.

'Oh, Wolfie!' groaned Gemma. He sat there with his head on one side and stared her out, refusing to move. She was late with his meat. Gemma went into the kitchen to open another tin.

She put the meat in the bowl and changed into jeans and trainers. For some reason, the new haircut made her walk in a different way. There was a slight swagger. Her head seemed to float above her shoulders and now, there seemed no reason to stare down at the ground in an apologetic way.

She picked up the bowl of dog meat and was about to take it outside when the door burst open. It was her father. His face, deathly white. In his hand was the braid of hair. He held it at arm's length, glared at Gemma and shook it in her face.

'What the hell have you done to yourself?' he yelled.

He'd never shouted at her like that before, ever. Her knees buckled.

'I...didn't think you'd mind. I...I thought it would help.'

'You could have cut yourself with the scissors! You could have... it looks...'

He was lost for words, then: 'How am I supposed to look after you, if you're just going to do your own thing?' He thumped the table. 'I've looked after you all these years and I've looked after you on my own and I thought I could trust you, Gemma!'

'You *can* trust me, Dad. I...'

'No! You've cut all your hair off. Was it because of the plaits? I can do plaits!'

'They were fine, all I was trying to...'

But he wasn't listening.

'I thought you were dead! I saw your hair hanging out of the dustbin. I thought you'd been murdered.'

She wrapped her arms round him. He was shaking.

'Daddy, I'm here. I'm safe,' said Gemma. 'I'll stay by you all through the holidays, like you said.'

He turned his face away. She knew she wasn't allowed to see him cry and found an excuse to leave.

'Is it all right if I feed the dogs now?' she said.

He nodded and gulped into his sleeve. Gemma touched his shoulder lightly, picked up the bowl of dog meat and went outside. The lid was off the dustbin. Wolfie had his great, hairy head in it and was rooting around noisily for scraps.

Gemma whistled to him, put the bowl down and sat on the steps. He wasn't interested. He'd found a spare rib and ran off down the street, tossing it in the air and catching it with a clunk in his great jaws.

Out of the corner of her eye, Gemma saw something move. Something hunched up under a car near the kerb. Gemma crouched down.

'C'mon,' she clicked. 'C'mon.'

Slowly, the creature unfolded itself and crawled out

from under the car. It was the Saluki.

'Come, Duchess!'

Gemma picked up the bowl of food and put it halfway between them. The dog hesitated for a second, then waddled over to the bowl and swallowed the meat in great gulps. Gemma could see the puppies moving around as she ate.

'What are you doing round here, Duchess? It's not a very nice place, you know.'

The dog gazed at her with soft, intelligent eyes, wagged its tail and came over to her. Gemma stroked the place where its collar should have been.

'Go back to your posh house and have your babies,' she said. 'Go on, go home.'

But Duchess had other plans. When Gemma picked up the empty bowl and walked back to the flat, Duchess followed.

Chapter Two

'Come on, Gem, we'll be late!'

Jim Diamond watched as his daughter settled the stray Saluki into a large grocery box under the kitchen table.

The dog had camped on the front step all night. When Gemma went to feed her in the morning, she was behaving oddly so she carried her into the flat. Jim had folded his arms and told Gemma to take her back outside.

'But we can't leave her out there! She could have her puppies any minute.'

'What if she needs to go out?'

'I could come home and let her out at lunchtime. Oh, please, Dad! Look at her.'

Duchess was shredding a newspaper and trying to make a nest.

'All right, but she's not staying. If Kasheffi finds out there's a dog in the flat, we've had it.' He fetched a bowl of water and stroked the dog firmly.

'Good girl... where have you come from then, eh? I bet someone's missing you.'

It was about fifteen minutes' walk to the house where Jim was going to build the new drive. Gemma marched along beside him, carrying a bucket, a rake and a book. She'd had strict instructions to sit and read the book while he did all the work.

'And you mustn't go near the concrete mixer.'

'No, Dad.'

'Because it could have your hand off.'

'Yes, Dad.'

She was thinking about making Duchess a kennel. She knew dogs weren't allowed in the flats, but no one said anything about the garden. And it wouldn't be just an ordinary kennel either. She was going to build her a palace.

'Is that rake too heavy? Do you want me to carry it, Gem?'

'I'm fine.'

She would make the kennel out of Western Red Cedar. That was beautiful stuff, with a good, straight grain. You could use it outside and because it was a softwood, it wouldn't be too difficult for her to saw. She would line it with oil-tempered hardboard to make it completely waterproof. That's what her dad used to line outbuildings. Then she'd need to get hold of some roofing felt.

She was making a mental plan of the kennel frame. Should she use dowel joints or corner plates to hold it together? Corner plates were metal, so they'd be stronger...

'Hold my hand, Gem. Look right, look left...'

He took the rake and the bucket and gripped her hand firmly as they crossed the road. She didn't complain, but the humiliation was dreadful. Ten years old and having to hold your dad's hand crossing the road!

The woman who needed the new drive was waiting for them at the door.

'Mr Diamond? Hello! Is this your son?'

Gemma grinned. She did look very like a boy with her cropped hair and workclothes.

'No, this is my daughter, Gem.'

'Jim?'

It did sound a bit like Jim, the way he said her name. She smiled at the woman.

'I'm Gemma.'

'I like short hair on a girl,' said Mrs Ellis. 'You don't want it long in this weather. Were you able to bring some identification, Mr Diamond?'

Jim showed her his library ticket and an old, paid gas bill. 'Sorry, I don't have a passport,' he said. 'Never been abroad, as it happens.'

'What, never? Oh, you don't know what you're missing,' she said. 'Anyway, doesn't matter, this'll do fine.' She twisted her apron. 'Sorry to even have to ask, but I was conned once. Made me a bit nervous.'

She pulled a sheepish face and ushered them into the kitchen. 'Come through . . . come through!'

Gemma watched as she made a pot of tea. The kitchen was much bigger than theirs with proper matching cupboards. And the tiles had no cracks in. There were fresh flowers, dried flowers, herbs in pots and a string of real onions hanging from a hook.

'Sugar, Mr Diamond?'

'Two, thanks. It's all right if Gem stays on site, is it? She won't be any bother, just going to read her book, aren't you?'

Gemma nodded.

'That's fine,' said Mrs Ellis. 'I'll put a chair out, Gemma, and if you get too hot, you come in, dear! Which book are you reading?'

Gemma showed her.

'It's about dogs.'

'I like dogs.' Mrs Ellis smiled. 'They're like humans, aren't they? Only nicer.' Gemma was going to tell her about Duchess when the doorbell rang.

'Oh, good. The concrete mixer's arrived... and the hardcore, I hope. Mr Diamond, could you check they've brought enough? Only Norman organised that side of it and we don't want to be a bag short, do we?'

Gemma followed her father outside.

At eleven-thirty precisely, a gold Mercedes with smoked glass windows drew up outside the flats and parked. A man in a brown leather jacket climbed out of the back seat and opened the driver's door.

Mr Kasheffi emerged, brushed the lapels of his immaculate suit with his gloved hand and looked his property up and down from the pavement.

He wore a ring the size of a grape over his right glove which he twisted rhythmically, as if he was trying to crack the code on a safe.

The sun glinted off everything he possessed; his bullion of a car, his preposterous emerald, and his oiled hair. It would have gleamed off his shoes which had been buffed to a blinding shine, but the effect was ruined by the transparent plastic bags he wore over them, secured with bicycle clips.

Mr Kasheffi believed poverty was contagious. He was terrified of it and did everything to avoid catching a dose. He turned to his henchman and clicked his fingers, his latex gloves muffling the signal.

'What are you waiting for, Milo? Fetch the rats.'

Milo undid the boot. He brought out a small sack which once held turnips. It was wriggling. Kasheffi took a green, silk handkerchief from his breast pocket and clamped it over his nose and mouth.

Together, they walked up to the main entrance to the flats, Milo keeping a nervous distance from the stout, sweating figure of his boss. Mr Kasheffi took a key, opened the door and let Milo in.

'Put them through the letterbox,' he said. 'Ground floor.'

Milo nodded.

'And Milo…'

'Sir?'

'Don't screw up.'

Mr Kasheffi turned and made his way slowly back to the car.

Gemma had finished reading her book already. She'd picked up some useful tips on how to look after puppies and now she was concentrating on the cement mixer. It was a friendly-looking, orange machine that seemed to have a personality of its own. It reminded her of Wolfie in a way. You had to keep feeding it to make it happy, and it was a noisy eater.

It was simple enough to operate. All you had to do was switch it on, put in half sand and aggregate and add water. Then you let the drum spin for thirty seconds until it took on the texture of stiff pudding mixture. It was just like making a cake.

'What next, Dad?'

'I need to bung in the rest of the sand, aggregate and water and give it about twenty minutes.'

Just then, Mrs Ellis came out. She gave Gemma a can of Coke and a plastic beaker.

'Mr Diamond, I've got the brochure for my bricks. I'm not sure which would be best for my garden wall. Could you spare me a minute?'

'Be right with you.'

He wiped his hands on his overalls.

'You be all right, Gem? Not too hot?'

'I've got a cold drink thanks, I'm fine.'

While he was gone, the concrete mixer stopped. Gemma was bored. It seemed silly to waste time when she could be helping. She stood up, put a load of sand on the shovel and fed it into the mixer's open mouth. It wasn't too heavy. She knew the right way to shovel something without hurting your back because she'd been watching an expert.

She started to spoon-feed the mixer with aggregate. It was hard work, but there wasn't that much of it and it was so exhilarating, the pain was almost pleasant.

'There's your... pudding!' she said.

She dashed the rest of the water from the bucket into the mixture with a satisfying slosh.

'And your drink!'

She pressed the button. The fat belly of the drum began to turn and the mixture slopped and smacked against the crusty sides, digesting its huge meal.

Gemma took out a stubby pencil and began to design Duchess's kennel on a blank page at the back of her book. She needed to get a tool kit together of sorts. Dad had most of the equipment.

She'd often rooted through his toolbag when he was elsewhere, cutting secret experiments out of scraps of wood, changing the bits on his drill, trying out the different grades of sandpaper on various objects round the house. But would he let her borrow it? Never! He would insist on making the kennel himself so she wouldn't cut herself or get a splinter.

This had to be *her* gift to Duchess. A home she could be happy in, so she'd want to stay. Every dog needs its own front door, she thought to herself. She wrote a note at the bottom of the page. 'Tools needed: Padsaw, G. Clamp, Hand Drill.'

'Gem!'

'Hello, Dad.'

'Gem... what did I tell you about the concrete mixer?'

'Um... add the sand, aggregate and water and mix for twenty minutes.'

She looked at her watch. 'Another fifteen and it should be done, I think.' She gave him a small, hopeful smile and carried on with her sketch.

'You loaded all that sand and all that aggregate?'

'Yes.'

'With that shovel, while I was in there with Mrs Ellis?'

'Yes.'

'Gem, look at me please.'

Their eyes met. This time, she didn't lower her head.

'Don't ever do it again,' he said. But he was trying not to smile. That little act of defiance had shown him she wasn't quite as delicate as he thought. Nevertheless, he still felt he was right to protect her.

'That thing could have had your... '

'Hand off,' said Gemma. 'But it didn't, did it? Because I'm not stupid.' She snapped her book shut.

'All right, Haircut,' he said. 'I tell you what. We'll nip home, feed the dog and then you can help me tip this lot into the wheelbarrow.'

Gemma looked up at him, hardly daring to believe it. 'Really? Can I really?'

'Blimey,' he said. 'It's only a bucket of cement. It's not as if it was Christmas.'

As they walked towards the flats, Gemma heard barking. She frowned and broke into a run.

'Dad . . . it's Duchess. There's something wrong!'

'Wait, Gem! It might be a burglar.'

He hurried past her and scanned the front of the house. The main entrance hadn't been kicked open and there were no obvious signs of a break-in.

'Maybe they got in through the back . . . no, stay there, Gem.'

He returned seconds later.

'No . . . nothing,' he said. 'Maybe she's hurt herself.'

He fished in his pockets for his keys and they went inside. They could hear Duchess hurling herself against the inside door to their flat. She sounded hysterical.

'Quick, Dad! She could be having a fit.'

'Stand back, in case, Gem.'

He rattled the key in the lock and pushed the door open. A rat ran over his foot and shot into the hallway. Duchess sprang after it, cornered it. It screamed and jumped at her face, clinging to her snout with all four paws. Jim held Gemma back by her arm.

'Leave her!'

'But it's sinking its teeth in!'

Duchess yelped.

'Get my leather gloves, Gem . . . quick!'

Leather gloves . . . leather gloves . . . where were his leather gloves? Gemma ran into the kitchen. There was a dead rat lying by the oven. She hardly took it in, desperate for the leather gloves . . . there they were, in the peg bag! She grabbed them, ran back. There was another rat lying on its back. It was bleeding from the mouth. When it saw her, it started shrieking and trying to turn itself over.

'Come on, Gem!'

'Got them!'

She turned her eyes away from the twisting rat, ran with the gloves and pushed them into Jim's hand. But he didn't need them now. The Saluki had torn the rat off and snapped its spine. Duchess backed off. Then, with a sharp whine she collapsed by the front door. Gemma tried to lift her back onto her feet, but she sank down again.

'Help me get her up, Dad!'

Together, they cradled the dog and carried her into the flat. The rat which had been screaming earlier was silent. Its eyes were fixed and glassy.

'There's another one in the kitchen,' said Gemma. 'How could they get in?'

They laid Duchess on the old settee. 'All right, Duchess . . . it's all right.'

Her wounds didn't seem too bad, but she was panting heavily. Gemma covered her with a towel and tried to clean the blood off her nose, but now Duchess was panting and licking herself under the tail.

'Dad, I think she's going to have her puppies. Shouldn't we call a vet?'

Jim reappeared with a dustpan. He scooped a rat off the carpet and dropped it into a plastic bag.

'Not yet... see how it goes. It's a natural thing, isn't it?'

'But what if they're not ready to be born?'

He threw his hands up. 'Look, I'm not being horrible but if I don't get back to the site, we'll have lost that batch of concrete. I can't afford to lose this job.'

Gemma stroked the dog's muzzle. 'You go back,' she said. 'I'll stay with Duchess.'

'No way. It's not safe. Those rats were put here, Gem. See this?' He showed her the turnip sack. It was in shreds. 'Kasheffi,' he said. 'He's trying to scare us out of here.'

'Please, Dad. I can't leave her all by herself!'

He looked at his watch. 'No, if anything happened to you, I'd never forgive myself. Come on, darling.'

Gemma rearranged the towel around Duchess and stood up, angry tears in her eyes.

'And if anything happens to *her*...' she blurted.

But the look on Jim's face stopped her finishing the sentence.

Chapter 3

The thrill of helping with the drive had been ruined. There was a constant nagging in the back of Gemma's mind that Duchess might be suffering and it made it difficult to concentrate.

Yet she must. If she messed up now, that would be it. Her father would think she couldn't do it and she'd be back in the chair, reading her book.

They'd tipped the mixed concrete into the wheelbarrow and while he dumped it on the hardcore, she was allowed to spread some over with the back of the rake.

'That's it, Gem . . . push and pull with it. Make sure it goes right into the corners.'

It was like icing a cake. He finished off the sections she couldn't reach and checked it over.

'What you looking for, Dad?'

'Making sure the cavities are filled. If you get air-pockets it'll weaken the concrete.'

She spotted a gap. 'That bit needs filling over there. Shall I press it down with the shovel?'

'Use your shoe.'

Later that afternoon, they sat on Mrs Ellis's front step with tea and biscuits and admired the new drive. The concrete was hardening off now. They'd tamped it with a long beam held between them – lifted it and dropped it, lifted it and dropped it all the way down, creating hundreds of ripples across the surface.

'You sure it's not too heavy?' he'd said.

''Course not.'

Her back was throbbing, her thighs were aching but being allowed to help was worth any number of strained muscles.

'Can we go now, Dad?'

He knew what she was thinking, because he was thinking the same thing.

'She'll be all right, Gem, I bet you.'

'Will she? Only what if the puppies are all right but she isn't and they don't have a mother? Will they survive?'

He put his arm round her. 'You did.'

'And you did,' said Gemma.

'I don't remember my mum at all,' said Jim. He dunked his biscuit into his tea thoughtfully. 'She died when I was a baby, I think.'

'You think . . . ?'

'I only know what my dad told me and he always clammed up about it, so I never pushed him. He was lovely, your Grandad Will, but he had a lot of depression.'

'Why?'

'Oh, he always felt he wasn't good enough. He never wanted to be a builder. I think he resented every brick he ever laid.'

Gemma couldn't remember Grandad Will at all, but he'd seen her when she was a baby. He was the one who suggested her name. 'She's a little Diamond,' he'd said. 'A little Gem.'

'What's wrong with being a builder?' she asked. 'I think it's wonderful, making houses for people and walls to keep them safe. Everyone needs a home.'

She couldn't understand how anyone could fail to see the importance of builders. Jim started to unroll a thick sheet of polythene over the drive.

'Yeah, but my dad had dreams of *living* in a mansion, not building one,' he said. 'Can you put a few bricks round the edge of this poly, Gem? Stop it blowing away.'

Gemma picked up a brick. 'If he thought being a builder was such a rubbish job, why did he make you leave school and be a bricky?'

'Oh, I dunno. Wasn't like I was going to get into university, was it? He said, "Jim, know your place. It's a waste of time trying to rise above it. Your ladder ain't long enough."'

Gemma tugged the polythene and fixed it in position with another brick.

'What ladder? What did he mean?'

Jim shrugged. 'Oh, he was just warning me against going after something I could never have, so I wouldn't end up disappointed like him. Just trying to protect me, I s'pose.'

Gemma brushed the brick dust off her hands and saw the beads of sweat already forming under the plastic sheeting. The drive was alive. It was a breathing thing, made from water and sand and stone. She had helped to create it, and in doing so, she'd actually made her mark on the planet. It was only a small mark, but the enormity of what she had done made her feel god-like.

'Nice job,' said Jim.

The sound of his voice jerked her back into reality. 'Can we go now, Dad?'

The walk home was much quicker than the journey there. There was no equipment to carry, they'd left it on site. They would go back tomorrow to finish off, then there was the wall to start.

When they came to the road, Jim held out his hand automatically and Gemma held it willingly, as friends.

'Thanks for letting me help,' she said.

'Thank *you*,' he insisted. 'I don't mean to baby you, Gem. Only what with me having no mum and no sisters, I don't really know all that much about...'

'Girls?'

'Who are they? I don't know.'

'Dad...?'

'What?'

'Can I borrow your tool kit?'

She told him about the kennel she was designing for Duchess. She got quite excited, thinking out loud about flat or angled roofs and the benefits of roofing felt over slates and he was chipping in with his own ideas, saying, 'Yeah, well, if you use my quarter inch cabinet screwdriver, that'll fit a straight slot screw, gauge eight,' and, 'How about using wood-faced ply? I've got a lovely bit of 4mm oak veneer.'

Suddenly, Duchess's Kennel Palace was no longer the stuff of fantasies. It was an on-going project. It was only when they got to the front door that this bubbling enthusiasm was dampened by a cold rush of dread. Maybe there would be no need for a kennel at all.

'I'll go in first,' said Jim.

'No... let's both.'

Jim took his dusty boots off on the mat, but Gemma hurried straight in. There was no sign of Duchess on the sofa. The towel was on the floor. Where had she crawled to?

'Gem . . . in here!'

'What? Is she all right? Is she . . . ?'

Gemma followed a thin trail of blood into her bedroom, her heart thumping. Jim put his finger to his lips.

'Ssshh.'

Duchess was in Gemma's wardrobe, curled up on her old duffel coat. Jim got down on his knees.

'There's three of them!'

'Three?'

'Look . . . one Duchess and three little Duchesses.'

Gemma crouched down. The puppies were butted-up like sausages, eyes closed, ears pressed to their heads. A small ginger one, an even smaller black one and a large, noisy, rusty coloured one that kept wriggling and squeaking and making a nuisance of itself.

'I bet that one's a boy,' said Gemma.

Over the next few weeks, the puppies thrived. Even the little black one was doing well. The rusty puppy was male, as Gemma had predicted and it was already twice the size of its sisters. He had already decided dog milk was boring, stolen Jim's bacon and eaten it in the bathroom. Gemma hadn't thought of proper names for the others yet, but she decided to call this one Duke.

'Duke?' laughed Jim. 'Are you sure? His mother might be a Duchess but I dread to think who the father was.'

'I think it was Wolfie,' said Gemma.

Duke certainly had a look of Wolfie about him. Duchess was tall, but she had a small, neat skull, a slender frame and a sleek coat. Duke was already a gangling handful of muscle and his fur was coarser.

'Seen my shoes, Gem?... Ugh!'

'What's up?'

'I've trodden in one again! The sooner these puppies go outside, the better.' He peeled his wet sock off.

'We'll have to find homes for them, you know.'

'Yes, but the little Duchesses aren't weaned yet.'

She was trying very hard not to get too attached to the puppies, but Duke in particular had other ideas. He took little notice of Duchess at all and decided that wherever Gemma was, that was the place to be. He even tried to get in the bath with her.

'Some of the girls at school might give them a home,' said her father.

School! Gemma didn't even want to think about it. No one at school had seen her new haircut and they were bound to think it was hilarious.

'Maybe,' she said. 'Or we could put an advert in the newsagent's. Good homes wanted.'

That way, she could choose the puppies' new owners. If she didn't like the look of a person, she wouldn't part with the dog. No way.

''Bout time they went in the garden during the day,' Jim suggested. 'How's that kennel coming along?'

The kennel was coming along better than Gemma had dared to hope. She'd been making it in the shed in the evenings. It had been slow-going at first, because the saw she'd chosen was too heavy and she'd cut some of the timber at the wrong angle.

She'd mentioned this casually at dinnertime and without saying anything, Jim equally casually left his tenon saw out on the kitchen table and went off to watch the snooker. The tenon saw was much easier to handle. She marked the timber properly this time and now everything fitted together like it was supposed to.

She was wondering about gluing it, but that meant putting the timber in clamps and waiting for it to dry and she was desperate to have a go with the hammer. It was a one and a half pounder, with a wooden handle. Jim wouldn't have a steel-handled hammer. If you hit the wood with the steel, it would leave a black mark, he said.

She practised on a spare piece of plywood, not the least bit afraid that she might whack her thumb. Driving a nail home was simply a matter of getting your arm in line with the hammer and letting it do the hard work. She talked herself into a rhythm...

'Support the nail, give it a tap, swing the hammer and bang!'

She'd been watching her dad do it all her life, so she was not altogether surprised to find she'd banged six nails in without bending a single one.

The last thing she needed to do was attach the door. She'd cut a beautiful, arched doorway using a hand drill and a padsaw, but as she was screwing it onto the hinges, she slipped and stabbed her finger quite badly. She swore and pressed the torn flap of skin back down, more worried about dripping blood on the kennel than the fact that she'd hurt herself.

There were plasters indoors, but she didn't want her father to know what she'd done, so she wrapped the wound in a tissue, bound it round tightly with duct tape and carried on.

It was getting dark. When Jim tapped on the shed

door, she nearly dropped her varnishing brush.

'Dad! You made me jump!'

'Do you now what time it is?'

'No... no, don't come in. I want it to be a surprise.'

Jim waited outside for her. She wanted him to go away so she could finish. The varnish brush had shed a few hairs and she needed to pick them out.

'Why... are we wai... ting,' sang Jim.

'All right, I'm *coming*.'

She snapped at him under her breath. Her head ached and the warm, night air made her feel slightly sick and she stumbled, knocking her injured hand against the old washing line post. The pain was excruciating, but she didn't dare draw attention to it. Jim steadied her.

'You must keep the door open when you're varnishing. The fumes are dangerous.'

'Window was open,' she said.

Before she went to bed, she managed to sneak a couple of plasters and tried to clean her finger in the sink. As soon as she unravelled the duct tape, it started to bleed again. She looked in the bathroom cabinet. Jim had a little white stick that he used if he cut himself shaving. She found it and pressed it into the wound. The pain made her head swim. She sat on the edge of the bath and held onto the sink until the dizziness passed.

When she got into bed, Duke was already waiting for her. Jim put his head round the door.

'Duke... tell Gemma what you ate today.'

Duke cocked his ears as if he was listening. Then he dived under the covers and stuck his wet nose on Gemma's leg. She squealed but she couldn't get him out because she was trying to hide her plaster.

'What did he eat? Tell me... not your bacon again, Dad?'

'He ate Mr Kasheffi's latest letter.'

Duke reappeared and barked. Jim wagged a finger at him.

'Don't say you didn't, because you did!'

'What did the letter say?' said Gemma. 'Same old thing, I suppose?'

Jim handed her several pieces of chewed notepaper.

'Oh, it's a jigsaw puzzle,' she grinned.

She laid it out on the duvet with her good hand.

'"Dear Mr Diamond, with regard to your complaint about the rats..." I didn't know you'd complained, Dad.'

Gemma panicked. Mr Kasheffi wasn't the sort of person you complained to. Mr Kasheffi's cleaning lady said he slept with a gun under his pillow.

'Of course I complained,' said Jim. 'Hey... don't worry! I was very polite.'

Duke snatched the next piece of paper and threw it in the air, snapping at it with his perfect teeth.

'Duke!'

Gemma tried to take the paper out of his mouth, but he'd swallowed it.

'It's all right,' said Jim, 'I've already read it. Kasheffi reckons he doesn't know anything about the rats but if there's a continuing problem, he'll deal with it... ha! And he says our tenancy expires at the end of next month.'

Gemma's face fell.

'But that doesn't give us very long! Where will we go?'

'He can't just throw us out,' said Jim. 'It's against the law.'

Unfortunately, Mr Kasheffi was above the law. Two days later, after the grand opening of Duchess's kennel, Gemma put the puppies out in the garden with their mother and left with Jim to help him build Mrs Ellis's wall.

A gold Mercedes pulled up. A man in a brown leather jacket and rubber gloves walked down the side of the house with a large bucket and threw lumps of fried chicken baited with rat poison onto the grass.

Duke, off his food after eating too much notepaper, was the only one to survive.

Chapter 4

Gemma lay on the rug with her arms round Duke and hid her face in his fur. Losing Duchess was terrible. Losing the two little Duchesses was a tragedy, but for Duke to lose his mother – that, she found unbearable.

She hadn't been able to cry when the vet came. They'd wrapped the puppies in old tea towels and he'd taken a quick look at them and shaken his head. Then he examined Duchess and said there was nothing he could do, it would be kinder to put her to sleep. She wouldn't survive the night anyway.

Jim sat with Duchess on the sofa while the vet prepared his equipment on the sideboard. Gemma wanted to hold her, but what she wanted seemed of no importance anymore. Duchess gazed at the floor while the vet shaved a small patch of fur from her leg.

'Why do that?' Gemma thought crossly. 'Why cut off her lovely fur?'

She touched her own short, spiky hair and looked at her father. His expression was distant, detached. The vet was about to fill the syringe when Duchess gave a low sigh and died.

'Ah...' said the vet. There seemed little point in getting his stethoscope out to confirm what was so obvious, but he did it anyway.

'She's gone.'

He suggested a post-mortem ought to be done on all

the dogs. If someone had deliberately poisoned them, it was a matter for the police. He could confirm what type of poison had been used.

Jim shook his head. The police wouldn't touch Kasheffi. He had friends in high places and say they did report him? The man had a gun. Jim wasn't afraid for himself, but for Gemma. She could end up fatherless.

He didn't have the energy to explain any of this to the vet. He just said, 'Doesn't seem much point.'

The vet insisted there was every point. What if it happened to someone else's dogs or even a child? Would they please think about that and could he at least take the chicken remains to confirm the cause of death? Jim nodded.

'Take the chicken,' he said. 'Leave the dogs.'

He buried Duchess with her pups at the bottom of the garden. He wouldn't let Gemma help.

'Go back indoors.'

She shook her head. She stood with her arms folded by the kennel. What a stupid, selfish empty monument it seemed now. What was she thinking of, trying to keep Duchess? She should have found out where she belonged and taken her back there.

Everything had its rightful place. Girls, dogs, bricks, cars . . . if they were in the wrong place, things fell apart. Walls fell down. Mothers got killed.

'Go away, Gemma. Please.'

He wouldn't look at her. She turned and as she turned, she kicked the kennel really hard.

She wanted it to splinter and collapse into useless, unidentifiable planks, but it wouldn't. She had made it too well.

She ran indoors. Jim waited for a while. He could sense Gemma watching him from the window and he turned round angrily, flicking his hand at her. 'Go *away*!'

He plunged the spade into the soil, snapping through the yellow, twisted roots of ivy. He dug deeper and deeper. He had never allowed himself to roar with grief when his wife was killed in case he frightened Gemma. He stifled the emotion until it fossilised into an ugly stone which embedded itself somewhere just below his ribs.

He hadn't cried for his own mother, because he didn't know what she looked like. There were no photos, no perfume, no places they'd been together. There was nothing to get hold of in his mind. He lowered Duchess carefully into the hole and knew that she was a mother he could mourn.

He arranged the puppies as if they were suckling, stood quietly for a moment, then covered them with soil. Then he scraped his spade clean, went into the shed and shut the door.

Over the course of summer, Duke came along in leaps and bounds. Gemma refused to part with him and Jim stopped suggesting trying to find him a new home. 'I can't wait until we move into our new place,' said Gemma. 'If Mr Kasheffi finds out we've still got a dog, he'll have us all shot.'

She was only half-joking. They had no proof, but they knew Kasheffi had killed their dogs. His defence would be that he was merely trying to poison the rats and that the dogs shouldn't have been there in the first place. In reality, he was determined to scare them out of his property as quickly as possible and he would stop at nothing.

What foul tricks he might have played to get rid of Mr Southam and the poor Spanish student they could only guess at.

'What use are the flats to him anyway?' Gemma asked. 'If he wants more money, why doesn't he just put the rent up?'

'Oh, he has,' said Jim. 'He's been putting it up and up. Last time, his minder came to collect it and I didn't have enough. If he knocks, don't open the door whatever you do.'

For the last few days, they'd been packing what little they had into cardboard boxes. Apart from the needlework box Jim had made for Gemma's mother, the rest of the furniture belonged to Mr Kasheffi, so there was nothing to put in storage.

'I wonder if it was him who burnt your van out after Christmas?' Gemma mused.

'I wonder! We'll get a new van soon, shall we?' said Jim. 'To go with our new flat.' He'd scraped together the deposit for a furnished basement about two miles away. It was near a park, which made it ideal for Duke.

'It's a bit pokey, Gem,' he'd said. 'But it's not forever, is it?'

Mrs Ellis was delighted with her drive and the way the wall was coming along and she had a friend opposite who wanted an extension built. Things were definitely looking up.

Every day, Gemma put Duke on his lead and took him to work. He liked to hold things in his mouth, so she let him carry the plastic bucket.

Once, she'd made the mistake of putting their sandwiches in it. They'd only gone a few metres when Duke realised what was in the greaseproof paper, dropped the bucket, rooted through the contents and sucked out all the cheese.

Gemma tried to tell him off, but he looked so ridiculous with pickles stuck to his eyebrows, she couldn't help laughing. They were definitely Wolfie's eyebrows.

Where was Wolfie, she wondered? He didn't come round anymore. It was an awful decision to have to make, but after Duchess and the puppies had been killed, she didn't dare leave meat out for the strays anymore in case rat poison found its way into their bowls.

Over the next week, the weather became humid and overly bright. Mrs Ellis's lawn had started to go brown in patches and there seemed to be too many leaves and hardly any flowers.

They'd nearly finished building the garden wall. It had been a massive job. Originally, there had been a wood panel fence all the way round, but this had lost most of its slats and some of the panels had blown down altogether.

'Anyone could get in,' Mrs Ellis had said. 'I don't feel safe.'

She wanted a solid, brick wall. It had to be two metres high all the way round. She would grow roses and berberis against it, anything with thorns to stop the bogeyman climbing over the top.

'You hear so many dreadful things these days,' she said.

Mrs Ellis was quite happy for Duke to be in the

garden while they worked. Gemma kept him on a lead which she slipped over a post while she was working. Until the wall was complete, he could easily escape into next door.

Gemma sat on the path and cut another brick. She drew a pencil line across it, scored it with a bolster and gave it a hard tap with a club hammer.

'That all right, Dad?'

He took it, turned it and held it loosely against the gap in the wall.

'Nice one,' he said. He balanced it on his huge palm, spread it with mortar as if he was buttering a slice of bread and laid it in position.

'We need to mix some more mortar.'

Gemma fetched her spade and measured the sand, cement and hydrated lime onto the mixing board.

Duke woke up. He'd been dozing quite happily under a crab apple tree with his head on his paws, but now he was hungry. He was about to run across the lawn to butt Gemma in the back of the knees when he was pulled up short by his lead.

He sat down sharply. He took the lead in his mouth and started worrying it. It felt nice and rough against his gums. He started pulling it through his teeth, rasping through the orange fibres.

Jim made a crater in the middle of the dry mortar pile and Gemma poured water slowly into the powdery hole with the plastic watering can. Her face was streaked with brick dust where she had wiped the sweat away.

'Why don't you go and sit in the shade, Gem?'

'No.'

'You must be hot. I know I am. I'm roasting,' he said.

She splashed some of the water over his leg deliberately and he jumped back, laughing.

'Oi! Pack it in.'

'Thought you were hot.'

He grinned and started to work the mortar into the water with his spade.

'Go on,' he said. 'I'll do this bit. About time Duke had his dinner, isn't it? How many does he have a day now? Ten, is it?'

'Four!'

She leant her spade against the wall and called cheerfully. 'Duke... Duke?'

He wasn't there. The lead was lying on the grass, chewed right through.

'Come on, come out. Where've you gone?'

She looked in the shed and behind the shrubbery. She slapped her knees and called again.

'Duke... Come on!'

She was starting to get concerned. 'I can't find him, Dad.' She held up the lead.

'He's probably gone inside. Have a look.'

Mrs Ellis rattled her biscuit tin and looked under all the beds, in the hall cupboard, everywhere.

There was no sign of him.

'He must have gone through the wall!' worried Gemma. 'He could be anywhere!' She ran back outside and looked through the gap into the next garden, but he wasn't there.

'Duke... *Duke*!'

'He can't have gone far,' said Mrs Ellis. The doorbell rang. 'Excuse me a minute...'

It was the woman over the road who wanted the

extension built. She was furious. There was a big dog in her garden trying to kill her son's guinea pig. Did it belong to the builder? Would somebody come and get it *now*!

Gemma went to collect Duke while her father apologised to the woman and promised it would never happen again. He was only a puppy. He'd eaten through his lead. The woman wasn't very sympathetic.

'What about our guinea pig?' she said. 'He nearly scared it to death.'

The guinea pig didn't look scared to Gemma. Duke wasn't trying to kill it. He was fascinated, that was all. Whenever it tried to walk past him, he leapt into the air, all four feet off the ground, then shoved his nose under it and flipped it over. It grumbled a bit, then pottered off and sat down in a clump of purple geraniums.

'Duke, leave!'

He turned and bowled over to Gemma, wagging his tail in happy circles, a few centimetres of frayed lead swinging from his collar. She led him out through the open back gate, over the road and back to Mrs Ellis's.

'She shouldn't have left her gate open,' said Mrs Ellis. 'It's her own silly fault. She should be grateful it was Duke who got in, not a burglar.'

Nevertheless, the next day, Jim decided it would be better to leave Duke in the flat.

Gemma disagreed. 'He hates being shut in, Dad. You know he does!'

But Jim wasn't budging. 'It's only for this morning while we finish the wall. It's not safe for him on-site. He could have got killed crossing the road into that woman's garden.'

'Okay. I'll get him a stronger lead.'

'Gem, it's only for one morning. If we go now, we can finish the wall, come home, feed Duke and clear out of here. Kasheffi wants us out by noon anyway.'

Gemma left Duke some extra meat for breakfast. He was growing so fast, it seemed impossible to fill him up. He was almost as tall as Duchess had been and he still had a long way to go before he grew into his feet. She ruffled his head.

''Bye, Duke. See you soon.'

Before they left, she checked her bedroom to make sure she'd packed everything she needed to take. It was strange to think she would never wake up in this bed again.

It was ten minutes to twelve. Mrs Ellis's wall still wasn't finished. Gemma tapped her watch and stood on one leg, then the other.

'Dad... look at the time.'

Jim wasn't ready. 'Yeah all right, I can't leave it like this, can I?'

She wanted to get Duke out of the flat before Mr Kasheffi arrived. If she bumped into him, she was afraid she might hit him with a spade for murdering Duchess.

'I could go by myself. If I run, I can get there before twelve, grab Duke and wait for you by the bus stop with the suitcases.'

He stopped scraping his mortar board and thought about it for a second.

'No. Anyway, those cases are far too heavy.'

'They're not. Come on, Dad. You know I can look after myself! I built this wall too, didn't I?' She could feel her voice getting higher and higher.

'Yeah, with me here to make sure you're doing it safely. You're talking about crossing the road. You're not exactly streetwise, are you?'

She was glaring at him. 'And I'm never *going* to be, am I?' She looked away, biting her lip.

'Now, stop it. I'll come now, okay? I'll leave all this . . . '

He waved angrily at the unfinished brickwork. There was only a short section left to do and he was annoyed with himself for not having finished – he'd promised Mrs Ellis. Now he'd have to come back after they'd moved flats and mix a fresh batch of mortar.

He walked in silence most of the way home, then Gemma couldn't bear it any longer and slipped her arm through his. He pretended to pull away.

'Gerroff . . . '

'No. Don't struggle. You might get run over.'

'Har-dee-Ha.'

They both relaxed. She was twittering away to him. How long was it going to be before he let her off the lead? She wouldn't run off like Duke, she laughed. What was the new flat like? Could she paint her own bedroom.? She wanted it to be yellow . . . no, green . . . no . . .

Suddenly, Jim stopped. He looked confused. He put his hand out automatically to protect her.

'I don't believe this . . . ' he said.

'What, Dad? *What*?'

The windows of their flat had been boarded up. The front door was padlocked and chained.

Duke was trapped inside.

Chapter 5

Gemma pushed past her father.

'We have to break in!' She went over to the window and tried to wrench the boards out of their nails.

'Don't!' Jim looked over his shoulder and lowered his voice. 'It's too dangerous.'

'Don't keep saying that!' she screamed. 'Duke's in there, we've got to get him out!'

Her hands were bleeding.

'Look!' said Jim, holding her hand close to her face. 'See what you've done?'

'It doesn't hurt. That's *our* flat, Dad!' She was outraged. Jim looked at his watch.

'No, it isn't. Not any more. It's gone twelve! It's Kasheffi's now. Surely he could have waited a few minutes? If that silly woman's wall had been a metre and a half high instead of two, we could have been here!'

He didn't seem to know what to do.

'Dad!'

Why was he just standing there? They couldn't leave Duke in there! So what if Mr Kasheffi had a gun? He wouldn't shoot them in broad daylight, would he?

She ran down the side of the house. Maybe the windows at the back weren't boarded up. Maybe they could kick the kitchen door in.

It was padlocked. She booted it with her foot in frustration. Jim pulled her away.

'You'll never do it, Gem! Stop, you'll break your ankle!'

'You do it, then!'

'No. Too noisy.' He examined the boards on the lower window. 'Find something in the shed to lever this up,' he said. 'A big screwdriver would do.'

Gemma ran to the bottom of the garden. She scanned the collection of tools hanging on the wall. Saw, trowel, hosepipe. No use. There were some others in an old coal scuttle in the corner. She tipped the lot out. A dusty spider ran across her hand as she grabbed a poker, a chisel and a pair of rusty pincers.

Jim had already managed to loosen a corner of one of the boards and was trying to tear it away. She handed him the pincers to force out the nails, but the heads were too small to grip.

He took the chisel, fidgeted it under the nail head and gave the handle a couple of upward blows with his fist. The nail popped out and he pulled the board away.

'Mind yourself.'

Duke came to the window. He put his paw up and ran his claws down the glass, delighted to see them. Gemma put her hand on the pane and patted it.

'It's all right, Duke.'

'I'll have to jemmy it,' Jim said. 'I can't smash it with him standing there. Just as well the wood's rotten.'

He inserted the chisel blade, tapped it in further with the poker knob, put his whole body weight behind it and pushed. There was a splintering sound and the window swung open. Jim grabbed Duke's collar to stop him jumping.

'Blimey, he weighs a ton!' he said. 'I can't hold him

from this angle. I'll have to climb in and lower him down.'

'Let him jump!'

'No, there's nails everywhere.'

Jim put his foot on the sill, pulled himself in through the window and jumped down into Gemma's bedroom. He put one arm under Duke's armpits, the other under his belly and started to lower him into the garden. Duke, startled by this new game, blinked quizzically and hung there, like a fur rug.

'Cor, he's heavy! Got him, Gem?'

Gemma was just easing him to the ground when there was a sound of heavy foosteps coming down the path. Thinking it was Kasheffi, Jim panicked.

'Chrissakes! Run, Gem!'

He pulled the window shut and stepped back into the room. Gemma grabbed Duke's collar and darted behind a bush. She crouched down, hardly daring to breathe as two policemen and a woman constable charged into the back garden.

'He's in there, Sarg!' said one of the men. 'Just saw him move.'

There was a pause.

'This is the police. Can you come out, sir? We need to talk to you.'

Gemma pressed her face into Duke's collar. 'What shall I do?' she whispered.

He licked her cheek. The seriousness of the situation had not registered in his soft, baby brain. She felt she should stand up and say something. Tell them her dad had done nothing wrong, it was all Mr Kasheffi's fault. But the police wouldn't touch him, would they? He was beyond the law.

'Come along, sir. What's your name, please?'

He was trying to explain.

'It's Jim Diamond. This isn't what it looks like. My daughter's dog . . .'

'Save it for down the station, mate. Jim Diamond, I am arresting you for suspected burglary . . .'

'You're joking? But that's my flat . . . was my flat!'

'You do not have to say anything but anything you say may be taken as evidence . . .'

They were reading him his rights, just like they did in the films. It wasn't fair! Gemma stood up.

'Let go of him! He hasn't done anything . . . you let go!'

Duke started barking. He could feel Gemma's hand shaking on his collar. She was upset . . . afraid. He could smell it.

'That'll be the daughter, Sarg . . . All right, love. Come on . . .'

The policewoman walked over to Gemma with her hand out. 'What's your name, dear?'

Gemma started to walk backwards.

'No.'

The two policemen dragged Jim out through the window and slammed him against the wall. They were trying to put handcuffs on him. Gemma walked backwards faster. The policewoman had to break into a trot to keep up with her.

'No one's going to hurt you . . .'

'No! . . . Leave my dad alone!'

The policewoman tried to rugby-tackle her to the ground, missed and hit her chin on the path.

'Da . . . d!'

Gemma danced on the spot, petrified, unable to think.

'Gemmaaaa!'

Jim tried to break free to get to her, but as he twisted, he elbowed one of the policemen in the face. It was an accident, he hadn't meant to. Gemma needed him. She was frightened.

He pulled away and tried to fetch her – to explain that she should go with the policewoman, that she wasn't to run off, that he would sort it all out.

'It'll be all right, Gemma. Darlin'?... You stay there!'

The injured policeman wiped a thin trickle of blood from his lip and looked at his superior. He nodded and pulled a truncheon out. The two men charged at Jim, threw him on the floor and pulled his hands behind his back.

Gemma hovered for one second... two. The policewoman, who had been talking into a radio, started to inch towards her. Gemma turned and ran. She could hear the woman cursing under her breath as she pushed through the brambles. Gemma slid behind the shed, lifted the wire fence at the back and wriggled under. She held it up for Duke and he dropped down on his belly and crawled through like a soldier.

The policewoman was too big to get under the wire. She tried to climb over the fence but she couldn't get her leg high enough. She fetched a bucket, turned it over and stood on it.

Gemma didn't look back. She scissor-jumped the next fence, leant over and heaved Duke up and onto the flowerbed, his paws scrabbling against the wire. He stopped to cock his leg.

'Come on, Duke!'

The policewoman had given up trying to get over the

fence. She decided to outwit Gemma by doubling back and ambushing her in the garden two doors along.

She ran up the street, puffing into her radio. She passed two houses, headed down an alleyway and pounded up the garden path. But there was no sign of the girl or the dog. She looked in the shed. Under the wheelbarrow. Nothing. She flopped down by the cucumber frames, caught her breath and swore. Her tights were torn, she'd lost her hat and she'd bruised both knees.

She muttered into her radio. 'Nothing doing here, sir... try further up, yeah? Roger.'

She panted slowly back down the path and disappeared.

Gemma waited until the police van drove off. Then she pushed away the thick hoops of honeysuckle she was hiding under and jumped down from the shed roof onto the compost heap.

'Good boy, Duke, jump!'

He sank up to his knees in the soft grass clippings and gave a little bark. She put her hands round his muzzle.

'Ssshh...'

Nobody came out of the house. Gemma sat and swung her legs. The policewoman hadn't found them! She wanted to laugh out loud. She pretended for a few moments that it was just a game, that her father hadn't been carted off by the police and that by teatime, they'd all be together in the new flat.

As soon as Jim had explained the situation to the police, they'd let him go. He'd come and find her.

Gemma yawned. The heat and the excitement had got to her. Double checking to make sure no one was watching from the house, she let Duke into the shed, wrestled an old deckchair open and sat down.

'Lie down, Duke.'

He crawled under the shade of the canvas and panted rhythmically.

'There's a pond,' Gemma told him. 'You can have some water in a minute.'

She half-wondered whether or not to go round to Mrs Ellis's and explain why they hadn't finished the wall. It seemed rude not to, and she'd be frightened if there was a gap in it.

'No,' she thought. 'Dad doesn't like me crossing the road by myself.'

What with that and the possibility of being recaptured by the police, she decided to stay put.

Gemma gazed up at the shed roof and tried to decide what sort of wood it was. Cedar, most probably. It was damp in the middle where the honeysuckle had rotted the roofing felt. All round the edges there were little cotton wool balls full of spiders' eggs.

The window-pane was set in a groove and held in place with silver pins and there was a huge cobweb in one corner, decorated with geranium petals.

'Nice curtains,' mused Gemma. 'Do you like our new house, Duke?'

But he'd gone to sleep.

Ted woke up and rubbed his eyes. There was a wood pigeon on his bedroom window-sill, cooing monotonously. It was half past five in the morning. Flaming pigeons!

He put his teeth in and went to the bathroom. What

day was it? Hang on a minute, he'd got his pension yesterday, so today must be . . . ? Ah, what did it matter? Might as well dig up a few spuds before it got too hot.

He pulled his trousers on over his pyjamas and went outside. It was lovely that time of the morning, everyone still in bed. He picked up a slug and threw it over the fence.

'Go on. Go and eat someone else's lettuces.'

He went into the shed to fetch his gardening fork and nearly fell over Duke, who had sensed his arrival several minutes before.

'Aye, aye . . . ?'

The old man bent his knees stiffly, scratched the dog's ears, patted his back.

'He . . . llo! What are you doing here, eh?'

Duke slipped through his legs, bounded over to the pond and drank noisily. Gemma stirred under the tarpaulin she had pulled over herself and sighed. Ted stepped backwards smartly, hitting the back of his head on the low shed door.

'Ow!'

Gemma sat up with a start and stared at Ted, wide-eyed. He was pointing his fork at her, like a bayonet.

'What you doin' in my shed?'

His voice was high-pitched with excitement. Gemma blinked at him sleepily and tried to figure out the answer. Suddenly, it all started to come back.

'What day is it?' she gasped.

'How should I know?' he said. 'What are you doing in my shed?'

Duke came lolloping in and jumped on top of Gemma.

'Stop it,' she squealed. 'Stop licking! I'm not breakfast!'

Ted, realising he wasn't in any immediate danger, leant on his fork handle.

'He's hungry,' he said. 'Does he like carrots?'

'Carrots?'

'My Charlie used to like carrots.'

He dipped his hand into a wooden tray full of sand, pulled something out and tossed it to Duke.

'Baby carrot,' he said. 'Didn't get many this year. Carrot fly.'

Gemma wrapped her hands round her knees.

'Do you grow all your own vegetables?'

'Yes, mate.'

Mr Southam had grown lettuces in the garden in Gemma's flat.

'My dad said not to eat them because of the lead in the air,' she said.

'If the lead don't get you, something else will,' he replied. 'Does your dad know where you are, son?'

He was the second one who'd mistaken her for a boy. She wanted to smile, but the mention of her father put a stop to that.

'I don't know where my dad is.'

'Eh?...Oh!'

Ted rubbed his chin.

'What about your mum, then? Won't she be wondering where you are?'

'I haven't got a mum.'

Saying the words out loud made her feel desperately alone. She felt a big lump in her throat and tears coming, hot and fast and uncontrollable. Ted panicked.

'Aw, no! Stop! You'll have me at it. I haven't got one either.'

He tugged a clumpy, cotton handkerchief out of his back pocket and waved it at her nervously.

'Thanks . . . haven't got one what?' sniffed Gemma.

'A mother,' he said. 'I'm an orphan.'

He grabbed the hanky back and started to mop his own eyes.

'How old were you when she died?' sniffed Gemma, looking into his birdlike eyes.

'Sixty-eight,' he said. 'Mind you, she had a good innings.' He wiped his nose on the back of his hand.

'Want an egg or something? That's it, cheer up, lad!'

Gemma and Duke went into Ted's house. Some socks and pants were soaking in the sink and there was a faint smell of damp. Old pickle jars full of wispy-rooted plant cuttings covered every available surface. There was an old-fashioned larder, big as a wardrobe, stacked with light bulbs and papers and bric-à-brac. Only one shelf was devoted to food, most of it in tins.

'I've got this dog food,' he said. 'Charlie died before he'd eaten it all. Any good?'

'I'd rather have an egg.'

Ted frowned, then he grinned so hard his teeth came adrift.

'Very funny!' he chuckled, clunking his denture back into place. 'I'd rather have an egg . . . Ha!'

He undid the can slowly, forcing the ancient opener to bite into the metal with its equally useless teeth. Duke stood with his front paws on the kitchen surface, eyes glued to the revolving tin.

'What's your name then?' Ted said.

'Duke,' said Gemma.

'Not his. *Yours*, dopey!'

'Oh.'

Gemma thought for a split second, then she said, 'Jimmy Scar.'

'No, it isn't,' said Ted.

No, it wasn't, but if she told him her real name, he might go to the police. Say the police found her and her dad was in prison? Where would she go? She didn't have any relatives. They didn't have any friends. There had only ever been Gem and Jim. Gemma Scar. Jimmy Scar.

'It is. I'm Jimmy Scar.'

'All right then, I'm Ronnie Biggs. Where do you live, Jimmy Scar?'

'Down the road.'

She told him what had happened, about Mr Kasheffi boarding up their flat.

'He's a crook, he is,' said Ted. 'I've heard he sleeps with a gun under his pillow and I'll tell you something else for nothing . . . '

He put the meat on a saucer for Duke, filled a pan with water and put it on the gas.

'His daughter is married to the Chief Inspector's son.'

'Really?'

'You didn't know that, did you? ' he said, tapping his huge, pitted nose. 'Ah, you see.' He dropped two brown eggs into the steaming pan. Gemma watched them roll round in the bubbling water and told him about her father being arrested and the fat policewoman chasing her across the gardens.

'I was out all day yesterday,' he said. 'Went to

Ramsgate to see my sister, Doris. I missed all the excitement then, did I?'

'Mr Biggs... can they keep my dad in prison just like that?' she asked.

He rolled his eyes. 'I'm not really Ronnie Biggs. Ronnie Biggs was a train robber. Don't they teach you anything at school? I'm Ted. What did you just ask me?'

Before she could answer, he remembered.

'Keep him in prison? No, he'll get a solicitor probably and he should be able to get him out on bail. Unless he hit a copper in which case they'll have him.'

'He did hit one.'

Ted shook his head.

'Oh dear. Hard or soft.'

'He just sort of caught him with his elbow.'

'No, no. Your egg. Do you wannit hard or soft or what?'

'Oh! I don't mind... Ted, what's "bail"?'

He took a couple of plates from the draining rack and rooted round for egg cups.

'Bail? If someone's arrested, someone else puts up money so he can be released until the trial.'

'Dad hasn't got any money.'

She told him about Mrs Ellis's wall, how they hadn't been able to finish it. Ted caught one of the boiled eggs in a spoon.

'He's up a gum tree then, isn't he? I'm afraid it's going to be too hard.'

'For Dad?'

'I'm talking about the egg.'

He took his wallet out of a kitchen drawer.

'Tell you what. Go up the newsagent's and get me a

paper. Don't mind which, as long as it's not one of them big ones. Oh, and some milk, cornflakes, a tin of whatever the dog wants and we'll take it from there, shall we?'

He gave her a twenty-pound note. 'That's the smallest I've got,' he said. 'That's twenty quid that is, so don't go running off with it.'

Gemma felt thrilled but nervous. She'd never been to the newsagent's on her own before. It was no distance, only just round the corner. But there was a road. She'd never crossed a road without her father.

She caught sight of her face in Ted's hall mirror on the way out. The brick dust had streaked into a gingery moustache above her top lip. She pulled her hat forward and down over her eyebrows and steeled herself. She was Jimmy Scar.

There were no cars about, but for Gemma, stepping off the kerb was as scary as jumping off a diving board, knowing you couldn't swim.

'Duke, sit!'

She looked from left to right five or six times, then held her breath and dipped her toe in. She started to walk across, holding Duke by the collar. The road seemed to grow wider by the second. Any moment now, she expected a car to come screaming round the corner, knocking her legs from under her.

The relief when she reached the other side was immense. She ruffled Duke's fur excitedly. 'I did it! See, I can do it!'

She strode into the shop. The newsagent was still busy marking up the morning papers. He hardly looked up, just put her shopping in a plastic bag, stuffed a folded paper in and dropped the change in her hand, not even bothering to count it out.

'Cheers, son.'

Having mastered crossing the road for a second time solo, Gemma skipped back down the road full of enthusiasm, the shopping banging against her leg. Duke insisted on carrying the paper.

She had just turned the corner when she saw a police car outside Ted's house. The street was crawling with blue uniforms. She grabbed Duke by the collar and ducked down.

There was no going back.

Chapter 6

Gemma ran as fast and as far as she could in the opposite direction. Within half an hour, she was completely lost. At first, it was an awful feeling, but after a while she stopped panicking and went into a kind of walking trance with Duke by her side.

She spent all day trying to stay invisible, taking care to avoid busy streets, public buildings and other dogs. When there was no one about, they stopped to rest, but sooner or later, someone would appear in the distance and force them to keep going.

It was getting dark now. They came to a park. It had been closed since dusk and the gate was padlocked, but Duke spotted a gap where the railings were missing and squeezed through. Gemma thought it might be a good place to sleep the night and followed.

There was a children's playground nearby. She sat on the deserted roundabout with Duke, shared a few handfuls of cornflakes and drank some of the milk. She was just about to lie back and close her eyes when she saw a dark figure suddenly sit up on one of the benches. Whoever it was had seen them and was coming over.

Gemma felt her stomach tighten. She shoved the cornflakes and milk back into the plastic bag, slid off the roundabout and almost slipped, her legs were shaking so much. She ran across the tarmac onto the dark football pitch and tried to focus on the streetlights ahead. Was the man following her? She didn't know. How could she hear his footsteps on the grass?

'Duke... where's the way out?' she wheezed. She couldn't see the gap in the railings! He found it straight away, went through and came back again for her, thinking it was all a great game and racing down the street.

They spent the night on a deserted railway platform curled up together in a little triangle of sheltered space under the steps. Dawn came and Gemma was woken by a great rumble in the distance. It took her a moment to realise what it was, then seizing the opportunity, she walked stiffly to the edge of the platform and waited for the approaching train.

She helped Duke up, sat down on the nearest seat and put the shopping bag next to her to stop anyone else sitting there. Not that there were many other passengers – just a tired-looking girl in her early twenties re-doing her eye make-up in a small handmirror and an old man, who seemed to be asleep.

Duke sniffed the carriage with interest. It had a greasy, airless stink he had never come across before.

'Sit, Duke. Good boy.'

As the train rattled into a tunnel, Gemma felt her mouth go dry. It reminded her of the time she'd begged to be allowed on the rollercoaster at the end of the pier when she was five.

'No, you might break your neck. You might knock your teeth out. You might hurt your back,' her father had said. But she'd sulked so much, he'd given in and said all right, as long as he went with her.

She'd hated every second of that ride. As it speeded up, all she could think of was how extremely dangerous it must be, because he'd put the thought into her mind. She wanted to get off. She thought she was going to die.

'I'm afraid you'll have to sit it out until the end,' he'd said.

Now here she was on a new ride. She didn't know when it would stop, where it was going or if it was safe. She supposed she'd just have to sit it out until the end all over again.

She didn't have a ticket. It had all happened too fast. If anybody asked to see her ticket she'd pretend she didn't understand, like Ziggy.

'*Ich kann Sie nicht verstehen.*'

The anonymity of the train had been frightening at first, but now she found it soothing. People got on, people got off, nobody looked at anyone else. They stared into space or pretended to doze.

Someone had left a newspaper on the seat opposite. No one was watching, so Gemma reached over, picked it up and started to read. Suddenly, she shrank back down in her seat. There, on the second page, was a picture of a girl with long, brown plaits.

'**Dodgy Diamond's Little Gem Does Runner!**' screamed the headline.

It was her old school photo, the one her dad carried in his wallet. She read the story beneath with disbelief.

'**Gemma, aged ten, daughter of Jim Diamond, suspected of carrying out several burglaries with violence, escaped from the police yesterday and has gone on the run . . .**'

The police said Jim was of 'no known address' and suggested that he was using Gemma as his accomplice, like the Artful Dodger in *Oliver Twist*. They had spoken to a terrified Mrs Ellis who claimed he had posed as a builder and left the job unfinished.

Another witness told of an urchin girl deliberately setting a vicious dog onto her son's guinea pig.

Then there was a pensioner who said that a girl disguised as a boy had hidden in his shed and stolen twenty pounds.

A certain Mr Kasheffi had admitted that Mr Diamond had persistently failed to pay his rent and kept his flat so filthy, it was overrun by rats. He had also been breeding dogs on the premises and when he discovered the puppies weren't pedigrees, he'd fed them rat poison. He had also driven the other tenants out with his constant hammering and drilling late at night.

Naturally, Mr Kasheffi was obliged to terminate his tenancy, whereupon Mr Diamond became abusive and violent and threatened to shoot him. There was even a photograph of the gun which Mr Kasheffi claimed to have found when he boarded-up the flat.

It was lies, all lies! 'Mr Diamond was helping the police with their enquiries.' Gemma's eyes misted over. The newsprint turned into little, crawling flies. How could they say those wicked things about her father?

This was all her fault. If she'd just sat and read her book like she'd been told instead of trying to build a wall, Duke would never have run off. He wouldn't have had to stay in the flat. Her dad wouldn't have had to climb in and rescue him.

Ziggy said safe was boring. She never told her that if you took risks, it was other people who had to pay for them.

She thought about going back and giving herself up.

That would be the good thing to do. What were her father's last words? 'You stay there.'

If she hadn't cut her hair, if she hadn't built a kennel, if she hadn't crossed all those roads by herself, she might have weakened and caught the next train home. Now, it was too late to do as she was told. Think, Gemma, think!

She had no home to go to. If she gave herself up, the authorities wouldn't let her stay with her father. She would be put in a home for wayward children and Duke would be taken away.

She couldn't let that happen. Right now, the only obvious solution was to run away and hide.

For a while, she couldn't decide which was worse - the enormous guilt she felt for deserting her father or the fear of what lay ahead. Eventually, both emotions became too exhausting to think about and burnt themselves out.

By the time she came to the end of the line, she felt almost lighthearted. The train stopped, she got out and with Duke carrying the newspaper, they headed towards the exit.

Jim was hauled before the magistrates at three p.m. He'd hardly slept the night before. What little sleep he had was tortured by harrowing images of Gemma being run down like a hedgehog on a busy road. Gemma kidnapped and murdered. Gemma lost.

He had been interviewed by the police. He'd pleaded his innocence again and again but no one seemed to believe him. They kept asking him the same questions in different ways until he was so confused, he hardly knew who he was.

They wanted to know where he was on Tuesday the tenth of November at four thirty p.m., but that was over eight months ago. When he said he genuinely couldn't remember, they asked if he'd visited a house in a street he'd never heard of and stolen a quantity of silver and a Victorian clock.

'No!' he protested.

'Where were you then, sir?'

He couldn't remember. Probably at home with his daughter, helping with her homework.

'And could his daughter verify that?'

Of course not. Nobody knew where she was.

'I want my daughter!' he'd shouted. 'She's only ten years old. You've got to find my daughter!'

They said they were doing their best. They had taken the photograph of Gemma from his wallet and sent it to all the papers.

'But she doesn't look like that anymore. No one will recognise her.'

But when they asked him for a more recent one, of course, no such thing existed.

In the meantime, he was to calm down and tell them about the time he'd broken into a similar residence two miles away and gagged and bound an elderly lady before making off with a Rolex watch, a diamond ring and an eighteenth-century, bronze figurine.

'I don't know what you're talking about.'

He refused to say any more until he'd spoken to a solicitor. They'd suspended the interview and taken him back to his cell where he had nothing to do but sit on the narrow bed and reflect upon his evil ways.

The police had taken his watch, so he'd lost all track of

time when the duty solicitor arrived. He listened wearily to Jim's story, bored by his constant protests of innocence.

'Yes, Mr Diamond, but what we need is a cast-iron alibi. Tell me about the gun.'

'What gun?'

'The one your landlord found in your old flat.'

Jim laughed out loud.

'I haven't got a gun. Why would I have a gun? I'm a builder, not a cowboy!'

The solicitor wasn't smiling.

'To defend yourself, perhaps? I believe you and Mr Kasheffi didn't see eye to eye?'

Jim shook his head in disbelief. If a gun had been found, there was only one possible answer. Kasheffi had planted his own gun there when he boarded-up the house.

'Is that why you broke into the flat, Mr Diamond? To get the gun?'

'No, to rescue the dog.'

'I can try telling that to the magistrate, but Mr Kasheffi's solicitor is likely to suggest that you're not very keen on dogs.'

'What? We had a bitch recently that had pups...'

'Yes, and I'm afraid there is a suggestion that you poisoned them.'

The more Jim protested, the more the solicitor pointed out that unless he could come up with a witness or produce a sound alibi, it was pretty much his word against Kasheffi's.

Also, he ought to be aware that Mr Kasheffi was quite a pillar of the community. He had sponsored the local cricket ground and contributed to the restoration of some very fine paintings in the Town Hall.

Jim didn't have the gift of the gab. He was a shy, quiet man who wanted to be left alone to get on with his life, simple and dull as it was.

'I don't know what to say,' he confessed.

The solicitor tried to put words into his mouth, creating fictitious scenarios that might buy Jim some time while he scrabbled around for more evidence. Jim didn't understand the process.

'But that's not what happened,' he repeated. 'It's a lie.'

'This is no time to be honest, Mr Diamond,' said the solicitor. 'No time at all.'

Various papers were prepared, and when Jim found himself standing in the magistrates' court, he hadn't a clue what he was supposed to say or do.

In the event, not much was expected of him. He stood when he was told to stand, he listened when anybody spoke. He hung his head like a model prisoner when he was refused bail on account of suspected possession of a firearm, causing grevious bodily harm to a policeman, resisting arrest, his alleged threatening behaviour towards Mr Kasheffi and the serious nature of the numerous other crimes he was supposed to have committed.

Throughout the procedure, Jim didn't recognise the man they were talking about at all.

He was stunned by the picture they'd formed in their minds about him. He'd never stolen so much as an apple, not even as a child.

The solicitor had asked the magistrate to take Mr Diamond's upbringing into consideration. He called Jim, 'A motherless child brought up in near poverty by an illiterate father who suffered mental problems.'

Jim rose angrily to defend his father but was told not

to interrupt, as if he were a schoolboy fooling about in class. He was to be sent to prison until the trial. Did he have anything to say?

'What about my daughter? What will happen to her?'

She would hopefully be found, assessed by a psychiatrist and placed in a suitable environment until Jim was released or had finished his sentence, whereupon the situation would be reviewed.

But there was no suitable environment for Gemma, except with him. He had failed to protect her. Somehow he'd managed to lose his wife, his dogs and now his daughter. With that agonising thought in his mind, he was led trembling back to his cell.

It was getting dark. Gemma had been walking through the forest all afternoon and there was still no sign of the trees coming to an end. If anything, they seemed to be getting denser.

It wasn't like the woods where she used to live. She would sometimes take the bus up to the heath with her father and they would stomp through the leaf litter and she would be allowed to walk along the fallen logs, holding his hand.

Those woods were full of people, dogs, pushchairs. Everybody out to get a breath of fresh air. Sometimes they took a picnic and the two of them would try and find a spot away from everybody else and pretend they were in the middle of nowhere.

This really *was* the middle of nowhere. Gemma sat down on a tree stump and shared the last of the cornflakes with Duke. She took a mouthful of milk. It was too warm and was starting to taste sickly. She poured the rest into her cupped hand and let Duke lap it up.

If he hadn't been there, Gemma might have wavered. She might have given up and waited to die or be rescued, like the Babes in the Wood. Right now, in the absence of her father, Duke gave her someone to take care of, so she kept going for his sake.

She often believed that she was the one caring for Jim. Oh, he was great at all the practical things like fixing doors and carrying heavy objects. He was forever getting the vacuum cleaner out, regrouting tiles and putting the washing on.

It never seemed to cross his mind that it might be nice to have flowers on the table. There were plenty growing wild in their back garden and once, she'd arranged daisies with scarlet pimpernels and dandelions in a teapot which she'd found in the top cupboard. He'd told her off about climbing on the chair to reach it, but he seemed to like the flowers and said how nice it was to have a woman's touch around the place.

Gemma hadn't seen a soul in the forest since that morning. Twenty minutes after she'd wandered in from the road, a boy crunched past on his bike carrying a fishing rod over his shoulder.

'Nice dog!' he yelled.

He'd turned and grinned and Duke had gambolled after him, whereupon he cheerfully shouted, 'Yow! He's after me!' and pedalled off into the distance with his knees sticking out.

Since then, there had been nobody. Now that the sun had gone down, there was a moist chill in the air. Gemma found herself shivering in her thin T-shirt. She rubbed her arms briskly.

'Come on, Duke.'

Duke was still hungry. He had pushed his nose into the cornflakes packet and now he was tearing it to shreds. The annoying thing was, Gemma had a tin of dog food with her, but of course there was no tin opener.

'Don't eat the cardboard, silly!'

Gemma put the shredded box into the plastic bag, put her head down and walked faster. 'We need to be out of here,' she said. 'We need to find McDonald's.'

She had plenty of money left for hamburgers and a drink. When it ran out... what would she do then? By tomorrow, all this mess would sort itself out, surely? She'd buy a paper and see if there was any more news about her father.

Suddenly, Duke stopped. He pricked up one ear, looked over his shoulder and started to slink along on his stomach.

'What? What's the matter?' Gemma couldn't hear anything. 'Stop it, Duke.'

He darted into the undergrowth and ran on ahead. She quickly lost sight of him in the gloom.

'Hey, come back... *Duke*!'

She could hear him barking in the distance and scrambled after the sound, pushing away the branches that were trying to poke her eyes. She tripped, tore her jeans and gashed her knee badly on a stone.

Clutching her leg and whimpering, she found herself in a small clearing and there, tethered to a post, was the ugliest horse she had ever seen.

It was snorting at Duke, who was down on his hunkers, eating what appeared at first glance to be a very small, roast chicken.

As the moonlight filtered through the gap in the trees, Gemma's eyes became accustomed to the light and she realised that the giant horse-donkey was leaning against a rustic fence which surrounded the most bizarre dwelling imaginable.

It was so skilfully blended into the surroundings, it was no wonder she hadn't noticed it at first. On closer investigation, she noticed that the roof was made from large, waxy leaves. These had been overlapped like roofing tiles and secured onto a framework of branches over which hung a froth of dense, white flowers.

The walls were made from several thicknesses of animal skins, some of which still had fur on. As far as Gemma could tell, these had been stretched over a frame of saplings and secured with nails made from pieces of sharpened flint.

Enchanted by this fantastic discovery, she forgot to be afraid and was about to push open the heavy door when she heard a sharp, metallic click. She spun round.

'Freeze, or I'll blow your hat off!'

Chapter 7

Gemma found herself staring down the barrel of a gun. A bright green eye glared at her from beneath the massive brim of a mossy felt hat, lavishly trimmed with crow's feathers.

The woman stood in silence, her trigger finger poised. She was dressed in a heavily patched, panniered ballgown made of emerald velvet which had been chopped off at the calf and sliced from neck to hem, to produce a fitted overcoat like that of a highwayman. This was fastened under the bosom with a clever arrangement of brooches from which an array of hooks, scissors and other trinkets were suspended.

Beneath this fabulous garment, she wore a long riding skirt, a blouse with a pie crust collar and a wide leather belt. This was threaded through the handles of two very old, stuffed suede evening bags which sat on her hips like swollen bee sacs.

Had Gemma been held at gunpoint by such a crazy-looking person back home, she would have fainted with terror by now. As it was, the situation was so absurd, she assumed she must be hallucinating due to exhaustion. The gun, the old lady and the peculiar little shack couldn't be real, could they?

It was the mule who broke the silence. He suddenly threw back his head and guffawed.

'Quiet, Cecil B!' hollered the woman. She lowered

the gun. 'There, now. You've spoilt my aim.'

The mule responded with a long, wet raspberry. Gemma giggled and the woman wagged a gloved finger at her, like a schoolteacher.

'*Don't* encourage him!' she barked. 'You... why were you trying to break into my home?' Although she spoke gruffly, she had a very plummy voice. She looked Gemma up and down.

'Are you a poor person?'

Gemma wasn't sure how to answer, but it seemed an answer was expected.

'I wasn't trying to break in! I'd never do that. I'm not a burglar.'

'That's not what I asked. Are you a *poor* person?'

Gemma shrugged. It seemed like a simple enough question, but when she thought about it, the more complicated it became.

'How do you mean "poor"?'

The woman stopped frowning and smiled secretively.

'Ah,' she said. 'I'm glad you asked me that, because that means you're rich!'

Gemma didn't agree. She fiddled in her pockets, and drew out Ted's change.

'There! That's all I've got in the world.'

The woman peered at the coins in disgust, wrinkling up her nose as if they stank.

'That's far too much,' she said. 'Throw it away! Bury it! Ugh! Wash your hands.'

Believing the woman to be completely mad and not wishing to upset her further, Gemma wrapped the coins in the ten-pound note and flung it over her head into the bushes. The woman clutched her heart and caught her breath back.

'Hoorah!' she wheezed. 'You are far richer without it. Now you are free to purchase all the wonderful things that money cannot buy.'

The woman swished her coat tails and danced around the little moonlit stage of the clearing.

'But I need to buy some food,' insisted Gemma. 'I can't do that without money, can I? Food doesn't grow on trees, does it?'

She was beginning to regret throwing her money into the undergrowth like that. She was starving. The woman stopped dancing and looked at her incredulously.

'Of course food grows on trees!' she exclaimed. 'Trees are all the wealth you need. With trees, I have the best builder's merchants in the world. I have a greengrocer's with wonderful nuts and fruits, I have the best chemist in Christendom, I . . . '

Here Gemma interrupted. 'Chemist? How can a tree be a chemist?'

'Medicine!' said the woman. 'Medicine from the bark, from the leaves, natural chemicals to cure all ills.'

Gemma was wondering if perhaps she was a witch of some kind, for there was something similar to a cauldron by her front door.

'No gas bills, no electricity bills . . . ' she continued. 'No need to burn money. I have all the free fuel I need right here.'

She spread her arms, as if she was embracing the entire forest. Her fingers were long and elegant and the fingerless, handstitched, moleskin gloves she wore revealed highly buffed, neat nails, the shape of almonds.

'All wood burns,' she said, as if repeating a mantra.

'All wood floats. It can be carved into boats, gates, plates, cups, weapons and traps.'

'Traps?' said Gemma. 'What sort of traps?'

'To catch food of course. Out there is the finest food hall you can imagine. All of it free! You said you were hungry, didn't you? What do you fancy to eat?'

'A Big Mac,' sighed Gemma.

The woman looked at her quizzically.

'A big what? Is that a modern thing?' she asked. 'I know nothing of the modern world.' Here, she spat. 'I avoid it at all costs, materially, emotionally, financially...' She paused, then added, 'Romantically,' under her breath, waiting to see how Gemma would react.

Gemma, amazed that there was anyone left in the universe who hadn't heard of McDonald's, ignored the mention of romance and spoke about beefburgers, fries and shakes with great authority.

The woman listened carefully, then spoke. 'So, basically, it's a penny bun with a minced-up cow inside and a few pieces of greenstuff?'

'Well, yes. I suppose it is,' agreed Gemma. Put like that, it didn't sound nearly as appetising.

The woman picked up her gun eagerly. 'I'll make you one out of minced deer!' she announced. 'I know where there are deer. Follow me, bring your hound.'

The woman whistled to Duke who trotted obediently over and stood next to her, waiting for Gemma to move. Gemma quickly thought up an excuse.

'But my knee!' she winced. 'I cut it on a stone...I really don't think I can walk much further today.'

The thought of shooting the deer was bad enough. The prospect of forcing its corpse through some medieval mincer made her stomach churn. The woman noticed her reluctance and swept over to her apologetically without seeming to touch the ground.

'You must forgive me, but I haven't had a visitor in years. My manners are somewhat rusty. My name is Monti, and you are?' She extended her hand to shake Gemma's.

'Jimmy Scar.'

'Welcome, Jimmy Scar.'

Monti pushed open the door of her leaf-thatched dwelling and ushered Gemma inside.

The soupy, green interior was illuminated by several tallow and beeswax candles. These looked handmade, for they were very uneven shapes and the wicks weren't like any wicks she'd ever seen. They appeared to be made out of strips of bark and in one instance, an old bootlace.

In the corner was a large mattress made from a pair of heavy, ruby-coloured curtains which had been sewn together to form a huge bag and stuffed to bursting point with straw, some of which was poking out through the seams. This was supported by a large bedstead, made from stripped logs.

'Sit on the bed, Jimmy Scar. I need to fetch a cobweb and some puffballs.'

She really is a witch, thought Gemma, her eyes wandering over the shelves crammed with pots and jars full of mysterious ingredients.

'What's a puffball?'

'It's a fungus. It's a mushroom. You can eat them when they're white inside and when they're past the eating stage, they make wonderful penicillin. Two in one. Marvellous!'

She shook a small biscuit tin and showed her the contents. It was full of deflated, dried-up old mushrooms. The smell hit the back of Gemma's throat and made her draw back. Monti pressed the lid back on and pointed to Gemma's blood-stained trouser leg.

'We need to clean the wound first.'

Gemma didn't want to take her jeans off. She was wearing flowery knickers underneath and given that she was masquerading as a boy, she was convinced they'd give the game away.

'Could you cut them off at the knee with your scissors?' she suggested.

'I will do,' said Monti. 'I haven't got a dress to fit you after all.'

Gemma frowned. 'Why would I want to wear a dress? I'm a *boy*!' she said.

'If you insist,' said Monti, cheerfully. 'We're all pretending to be someone.' She unhooked the silver scissors from one of her gem-encrusted brooches and cut through the thin denim just above the tear.

Gemma was transfixed by her jewellery. When the candlelight struck against the stones, the sparks they threw out were blinding.

'Are those real diamonds?' she asked.

'I don't know and I don't care,' said Monti. 'I suspect they are. Father bought them for Mother and she wouldn't have been seen dead in paste.'

'Paste?'

'Pretend diamonds, Jimmy Scar! Fakes, worthless diamanté! Or diamont*i*, depending on one's accent. It was the inspiration for my nickname, you know.'

So she wasn't really called Monti?

'It's what someone used to call me. It was a little play on words which connected the two of us. I loved him, I lost him,' she sighed, 'but I will always keep his name.'

She stopped snipping and fetched a monogrammed, china soup bowl which she filled with water from a stone jar. She took a clean, linen handkerchief out of an old trunk, unwrapped a yellowish, speckled cake of soap and started to bathe Gemma's wound.

'I've never seen soap like that before,' Gemma said. 'Where did you get it?'

'I made it,' said Monti. She looked disapprovingly at Gemma's dirty hair. 'I also make my own shampoo out of nettle leaves. Good hygiene is one of the basic rules of survival.' She sniffed. 'If you stink like a tramp, the quarry can smell you miles away. You couldn't track a backward elephant.'

Gemma wasn't sure about the significance of the elephant, but she was impressed by the soap. It didn't look as good as the soap in the shops, but it smelled lovely.

'Lavender,' said Monti. 'It's a natural antiseptic. I mix the flowerheads with melted animal fat, burnt wood, crushed bone and plant roots, then I filter the whole lot through a pair of silk stockings.'

Gemma was intrigued by this magical concoction, but it wasn't just the recipe that excited her. It was the creeping realisation that here was a woman who also believed in the magic of conjuring things from nothing.

She gazed round at the architecture of beams and branches that held up the roof, the flat stones that made up the floor, each one chosen, dug out, lifted, carried and placed so purposefully in its new home. Monti had marked out her plot on the planet and recreated it to her own specifications. Gemma had found a soulmate.

When she compared herself to the girls at school, she sometimes felt she belonged to another species, or even another gender that had never been identified.

She looked like a girl with her long hair and school skirt but she never felt she'd quite joined the club. She couldn't get to grips with their mind games at all. She'd tried to join in with their giggling conversations about boys and fashion, but couldn't see the fascination of either.

She was much more at ease with the black and white behaviour of the boys in her class. While none of them were close friends, they never tormented her. They simply absorbed her into their group and let her join in without privilege. Although she didn't always agree with the way they tackled things, she understood where they were coming from. She'd studied her father for long enough. The ways of women she was less sure of. She had never been close to any.

Monti rubbed the soap into a thin lather. 'What are you thinking, Jimmy Scar?'

'Did you make the silk stockings, the ones you filtered the soap through?'

Gemma wouldn't have been at all surprised if the answer was yes. Monti seemed to be entirely self-sufficient.

'My lover gave them to me,' she said. 'He couldn't afford them, silly man, and I didn't want him to waste his money. I preferred to go barefoot in those days,' she added.

Gemma found herself blushing. Monti looked her in the eye.

'You can't imagine me having a lover, can you?' she continued quietly. 'You look at me and you think I have always been seventy years old. Ha! We ran away to Paris together!'

'You're *seventy*?'

Gemma had thought fifty at the most. Although her skin was a little loose at the neck, it was still taut over her high cheek bones and her posture was like a ballet dancer's – head up, shoulders back, stomach in.

'Well, that's what comes of Mother forcing me to go to deportment classes,' she snorted. 'I suppose I should be grateful.'

'What are deportment classes?'

'Lots of rich girls walking around with books on their heads learning how to look down their noses at the poor,' replied Monti, waspishly.

She was dropping all kinds of intriguing little clues about herself. Gemma wanted to know more.

'Who was your lover?'

Monty stared up at the ceiling.

'Cobweb!' she exclaimed. She stood up, fetched a long stick, wound the sticky, grey mass onto it like candyfloss and pulled it down. She laid it carefully over Gemma's knee.

'Don't move a muscle.'

Monti poured a a few drops of water into a small tin lid. She held the tin lid over a candle with a pair of tweezers until it was hot, then straightened Gemma's leg, sprinkled the water onto the cobweb and moulded it into the shape of the cut.

'What on earth are you doing, Monti? Haven't you got any proper plasters?'

'This is a proper plaster. Watch and learn.'

Monti took one of the imploded puffballs out of the biscuit tin and broke it in half. It was full of brown powder.

'Natural penicillin,' she said. 'It will heal the wound in no time. I used it when Cecil B cut his fetlock, silly old mule.'

She sprinkled the cobweb-covered gash with the mushroom spores and wiped her hands on her skirt. 'There, that should do it.'

Gemma flexed her knee. The medicine was doing its trick. The blood was clotting already and the pain was almost gone.

There was a whinnying noise outside punctuated by a series of short barks. Duke was clearly having some kind of conversation with the mule.

'Where did you find Cecil B, Monti?'

'I didn't find him, he found me,' said Monti. 'He'd probably been living in the forest for donkey's years . . . Cec . . . il!'

She made a clicking noise with her mouth and Cecil pushed his head round the door and rolled his big brown eyes. Gemma roared with laughter.

'He's so funny-looking!' she roared. 'He's hysterical!'

Monti wasn't laughing.

'Hark at you,' she said. 'Pots and kettles.' She patted the old mule on the nose. 'His mother was a racehorse and his father was a donkey. A pleasing combination, I think. *You* might think his parents wouldn't have a lot in common, but I would disagree very strongly and call you a snob of the first degree.'

Cecil B huffed down his nose at Monti and snickered softly.

'Oh, I'm not a snob,' said Gemma, hurt by the suggestion. 'Duke isn't a pedigree but I think he's the best dog in the world.'

She called him and he came bumbling in, full of life after a good meal and an invigorating nap. Gemma hugged him round the neck.

'His mother was a Duchess, you know.'

'Ah,' said Monti. 'He and I have something in common. Who was his father?'

Gemma rubbed the dog's ears affectionately and they butted heads. 'I don't know, but I'm pretty sure he was a stray.'

Monti sat down on the floor, crossing her legs neatly at the ankle. She took out a knife from one of the billowing folds of her coat and began to score a ring around a short length of sycamore wood. She looked at Gemma thoughtfully.

'Are you a stray, Jimmy Scar?'

Gemma sighed. 'Yes, I think I probably am.'

She told Monti about Mr Kasheffi boarding up the flat and how she'd made her father rescue Duke. She told her about the police and said she was afraid they'd never let him out of prison, even though he'd done nothing wrong.

'And it's all my mother's fault!' she sobbed.

She had admitted the unspeakable – she was furious with her mother for getting herself killed.

'Mothers!' sighed Monti. 'Even in death, they do us wrong.'

Gemma thought she was being sarcastic. 'What would you know?' she exploded. 'Your mother didn't die when you were a baby!'

Monti twisted the section of scored wood, cut a small

V in it and put it in her lap. She didn't look at Gemma, she just stopped scraping the end of the sycamore length for as long as the next sentence took.

'My mother was shot dead by my father while trying to defend her only grandson.' Gemma went silent. She mulled the words over in her head and tried to make sense of them. It seemed very few words for such a monumental event.

'Cat got your tongue?' said Monti.

'Your father shot your mother?'

Monti looked up. 'Yes – you haven't got the monopoly on scars, dear. Mine is on the inside and it goes from here to here.' She took the knife and drew an imaginary line from her breastbone to her navel.

'Your own father? That's monstrous! That's...' Gemma shuddered. 'That's *evil*.'

'No,' said Monti. 'He was neither of those things. He was a snob, plain and simple. He couldn't bear the fact that my child, the heir to his fortune, had been sired by a tradesman who could barely write his own name.'

Monti folded the knife blade back into its silver sheath. 'It went against protocol, you see. Under normal circumstances, Daddy wouldn't have harmed a fly.'

Gemma was confused. 'But he shot your mother!'

'It was an accident. He meant to shoot my lover when he asked his permission to marry me. Daddy grabbed his gun, I gave the baby to his father and told him to run, but he wasn't the running kind, you see?'

'And then...?'

Monti shrugged as if it was hardly worth mentioning. 'Then Mother threw herself across them both and... bang!'

Gemma's jaw dropped open. The old woman held a finger under the girl's chin and closed her mouth for her.

'Don't look so shocked, Jimmy Scar, mothers get themselves killed every day, careless creatures that they are. Fathers get sent to jail. Not sure to this day if Daddy died of a broken heart or a lack of decent caviar.'

'My father has never had caviar,' said Gemma.

'Then he won't die from a lack of it,' said Monti. 'My father was weaned on the stuff and when he found out they didn't serve it in prison, his body went into shock.' She took one look at Gemma's downturned mouth and reprimanded her. 'Be *happy*, Jimmy Scar, I'm trying to *comfort* you.'

She replaced the small section of bark she'd removed from the little wooden pipe and blew down it smartly. It sounded just like a duck. Gemma couldn't help grinning.

'What is *that*?'

'It's a poacher's whistle.'

Monti blew down the tube of wood again, producing a high-pitched shriek. Duke leapt up, eyes blazing. He started pawing at the door.

'He knows!' laughed Monti. 'That was a rabbit cry.'

'But he's never heard a rabbit cry!' gasped Gemma.

'Don't you believe it.'

She passed the whistle to Gemma. She rolled it in her hands. It was a beautifully crafted little thing.

'Can I have a go?'

Monti nodded. Gemma found it hard to control her breath after all the sobbing she'd done, but gradually she got a few squeaks out of it. Obviously, it would take practice.

‘Come on,’ said Monti. ‘I’ll teach you how to whistle for your supper.’

She picked up her gun and Gemma and Duke followed her innocently into the forest.

Chapter 8

In the few, glorious weeks that followed, Gemma learnt more living with Monti than she'd ever learnt at school. She felt as if she'd burst out of a chrysalis and transformed beyond recognition.

Her legs were stronger, her shoulders less rounded. Her jeans were looser round the waist. Instead of watching television and eating pizza, she had to hunt for her food.

Gemma hated the idea of killing animals, even though she liked meat. She'd dug her heels in at first and insisted on being a vegetarian. Monti said she could do as she pleased and offered to show her the fruit and veg section in the great, green supermarket of the forest. Duke went too, insisting on carrying the basket.

'What shall I have?' Gemma asked. There were no obvious fruits or nuts apart from a few blackberries.

'You can eat the leaves and bark from all trees except yew, laburnum and rhododendron,' Monti replied.

'Leaves and bark? Ugh!'

'Very nutritious,' Monti insisted. 'Personally, I'd go for the mushrooms. You want to look in dark, damp places for those . . . try under that log.'

Gemma gathered a few and put them in her basket. Monti picked one out and shook her head.

'No, no, no,' she said. 'That's a Death Cap – *Amanita Philloides*. Smell it and remember it. Swallow that little baby and it will probably kill you.'

'How?'

Monti rubbed her chin.

'Symptoms – you start off with a hideous bout of vomiting, followed by a splitting headache, dizzy spells, watering eyes, a general feeling of doom . . . '

'I feel like that when I have a maths test,' joked Gemma.

'. . . Your skin changes colour, your pulse slows down then you drop dead.'

Gemma looked at the rest of the mushrooms in her basket with suspicion. 'I'm not sure I want to risk eating these.'

Monti trod on the offending Death Cap.

'The rest of them are fine, but if you don't believe me, try some of those,' she said, pointing to a large clump of nettles.

'Nettles?' Gemma pulled a face.

'They're very good,' Monti insisted. 'They make nice tea and you can use the flowers to thicken rabbit soup.'

'I am *not* killing a rabbit,' said Gemma.

Monti looked confused.

'Why this sudden aversion to killing animals, Jimmy Scar? You were the one who wanted minced cow in a bun.'

'That's different.'

'How so? It's still a dead cow, isn't it?'

Gemma crossed her arms defiantly. 'Yes, but *I* didn't kill it.'

'No, but you ate it, Jimmy Scar! If you feel so badly about killing animals, you should stick to salad as a matter of principle.'

Gemma knew it was a fair point, but the prospect of

killing something furry still bothered her.

'I suppose I could eat eggs and fish,' she said.

'All eggs are edible' said Monti, 'and if you'd like to go fishing, I know a place.'

'But we haven't got a fishing rod . . . '

Monti pulled a slim bottle from one of her numerous pockets and waved it at Gemma.

'Yes, we have.'

'That's a bottle, Monti.'

'I don't think so, Jimmy.'

They walked for miles through the forest. Although Gemma was much fitter than she had been, the journey was starting to take its toll.

'I wish we'd brought Cecil B,' said Gemma. 'I'm exhausted.'

'We only ride Cecil B on long journeys,' said Monti, gaily. 'It shouldn't be too far for a great big girl like you.'

'Boy,' corrected Gemma.

'Whatever.'

Duke found the stream first. He ran on ahead, came back and shook the water out of his fur so vigorously he became a blur.

'I'm dying for a drink,' said Gemma and she raced off to the edge of the stream and filled her cupped hands with water.

'You will be dying if it's polluted,' said Monti.

'But it looks clean,' said Gemma,

'Always test first,' Monti advised. 'You don't know who's dumping what into where.'

The water looked so inviting, Gemma wanted to gulp it down like lemonade.

'Put your finger in your ear,' said Monti. 'Dig a bit of wax out.'

'Ugh. Why?'

Not for the first time, Gemma questioned Monti's sanity.

'Go on.'

Giggling, Gemma did as she was told and showed Monti the little amber blob on the end of her finger.

'Right, now fill your cupped hand with water and drop the wax in.'

It was some sort of test, like they did in science lessons. Gemma watched the wax sink onto her palm.

'Show me,' said Monti. 'Good, it's sunk to the bottom. That means the water is clean.'

'Really? What would have happened if it was dirty?'

'The water would have shown a colour spectrum. You know, like a puddle of oil does on the road?'

Gemma lay down on her stomach and drank. Then she filled her hat with water and put it back on her head. Water dripped off her fringe.

'Your hair is starting to curl,' Monti noticed.

'It used to be really long,' said Gemma, 'but I . . . I mean Ziggy . . . ' She blushed. She'd almost told Monti about the plaits!

'You cut it,' said Monti. 'I wanted short hair once, but I was in love and the silly lad didn't want me to cut it. Said it was my crowning glory! I thought it was so shallow of him. If he really loved me, he wouldn't care if I was bald.'

Gemma couldn't believe Monti would let any man tell her what to do.

'But I loved him,' she explained. 'I wanted to please

him, even against my better judgement. That's what love makes you do.'

Monti snapped a thin branch from an overhanging tree and stripped the leaves off slowly.

'There was no need for us to get married,' she argued. 'We were quite happy in our little blue room in Paris, just me, him and the baby.'

Gemma lay down on the grassy bank and put her arms behind her head. 'Why didn't you stay there then?'

'He wanted his son to have everything he never had. The pity of it was, he thought *money* was everything. Pah!'

Monty threw the ripped leaves up in the air in an angry gesture.

'The reason I loved him in the first place was because he wasn't full of himself like the spoilt oafs my father wanted me to marry. He was honest and passionate. There was no side to him.'

She rammed the stick into the bottle and screwed her face up.

'Unfortunately, he just couldn't believe I was happy living on a shoestring and that was our undoing. That's why I live like this. To prove him wrong!'

Gemma rolled over onto her stomach.

'But after your father died, he could have married you. You could have lived on your inheritance and everyone would have been happy.'

'Maybe. But *maybe* he thought I'd blame him for my mother's death.'

'And did you? *Do* you?'

Monti was conjuring a length of fishing line from the inner sanctuary of an unknown pocket.

'Don't be ridiculous,' she said. 'I blame my mother. Doesn't everybody?'

Gemma sat quietly for a moment, wondering how different Monti's life would have been if she'd married the man she loved.

'Do you miss him?'

Monti thought about it.

'I miss something. I'm not sure what anymore.'

'Male company?'

'No, I've got Cecil B, haven't I?'

'And me?' added Gemma.

Monti raised one eyebrow.

'Jimmy Scar, when are you going to stop all this nonsense? I knew you were a girl from the day I met you.'

'How?...*How*?'

Gemma was furious! How could she tell? Hadn't she behaved just like a boy? Hadn't she taken care to undress behind the door?

'Was it because I cried about my dad?'

'Good God, no. Men cry all the time. You've got the wrong leg shape for a lad, that's all. A boy in tight trousers hasn't got a gap between his knees and thighs when he stands up. I could see the moon through yours, dear.'

'No.'

Gemma stood up, clamped her knees together. Sure enough, there was the definitive gap.

'Oh, *Monti*!' she scowled.

'Oh, nothing!' said Monti. 'What's wrong with being a girl?'

'Well, now you won't let me do anything! I'll have to

sit and read a book and not touch anything sharp I suppose!'

Monti looked at the furious little face. It seemed so familiar and touched a chord so deep she wanted to put her arm around the child as if she was her own.

'Jimmy, *Jimmy*!' she said. 'It is not for me to say how girls or boy or mules should behave. You must do as you please! The only rule is, you have to take the consequences.'

That seemed fair enough to Gemma. She calmed down, stopped pouting and sucked a piece of grass.

'Is that what you're doing, Monti? Taking the consequences?'

'I should say so. Now, are you going to tie a bait hook on the end of this line or do I have to do everything?'

The bottle and stick rod worked a treat. They took the contraption downstream, wound the fishing line round the bottle, weight and hook and cast the line. Then Monti wedged the bottle in the soft mud on the edge of the bank and they sat and waited.

'Where did you learn all this stuff?' Gemma asked.

'What stuff?'

'About survival and everything.'

'Charlie Coggins.'

Monti looked heavenwards, with almost religious reverence. 'He was a poacher. He lived on my father's estate. I used to run away from my governess and go and find him. He taught me everything...'

She drifted off for a while, trying to picture her girlhood hero. Yes, she could still see him, blending against the dappled tree bark like a wood sprite.

'He taught me how to track when I was supposed to

be learning my Latin verbs!' she smiled. 'Ha!'

The fishing float dipped under the surface of the water. Gemma waved her arms excitedly.

'Look... look!'

'Go on then,' said Monti. 'Catch yourself a fish!'

Gemma had caught a bream. Back home, they were deciding how to cook it.

'Boiled, smoked or poached?' asked Monti.

There was a small mud oven to the left of the room. Its base was made from a flat stone, about thirty centimetres wide. This was built up with thick mud into which a hollow stick had been pushed to form a chimney a metre long, which disappeared out through a hole in the wall. Through the mud opening, it was possible to see the edge of another large stone which served as the oven shelf.

This was used for cooking all manner of delicacies from roast pigeon to baked hedgehog. Gemma decided she wanted the fish done in a pan in the open air, so while Monti got on with the gory business of gutting and cleaning it, Gemma attempted to make a fire outside in the clearing.

Monti had shown her several methods of doing this without matches, and after various disasters with glass reflectors and rubbing two sticks together, Gemma decided to try it using a flint and steel.

She had built her fire out of soft wood, because although it gave off rather a lot of smoke, it was quicker to heat than oak or beech. There would be fewer embers, but that didn't matter because the fish needed to be cooked quickly. She'd never had bream and couldn't wait to see if it tasted anything like fishfingers.

Monti was surprised to see how quickly Gemma had mastered the art of fire-building. By the time she came out with the prepared fish, the embers were glowing in readiness above the little platform of green logs that Gemma had built to contain it all.

'You certainly have a way with wood,' she said. 'I noticed earlier when you were using the axe as well. In the Girl Guides, were you?'

'No,' said Gemma. 'My dad's a builder.'

'A builder? That would explain it. I've always had a soft spot for builders.' She winked and then seemed embarrassed by the gesture and pretended she had something in her eye.

'I've watched him making things since I was little,' explained Gemma. 'But it's only recently he's let me use his tools. Always fussing I'd hurt myself.'

She told Monti about the kennel she made for Duchess.

'I wanted to build her a palace,' she sighed. 'Now I wish I'd made her go back home, then she'd still be alive.'

'She made her choice,' said Monti. 'I wouldn't go back to my palace.'

'You lived in a palace?'

Monti tucked some herbs inside the slitted bream and placed the pan over the fire.

'It was a mansion,' she said. 'Dreadful place. Beautiful, dreadful place.'

'Beautiful, dreadful?'

It was beautiful to look at, Monti said. She loved its curves and its sweeps and the way someone had bothered to carve little figures into the plaster.

'Mind you,' she said. 'It was a crumbling old pile even then. That's why Mother hired him, you see. That's how I met him. He was mending the roof.'

'Who?'

'My lover! I used to arrange myself on the lawn, tossing my hair and thrusting out my bosom in the hope that he'd notice me. Don't look at me like that, Jimmy Scar. Watch the fish doesn't burn!'

'So, Monti. Did he climb down the ladder and ask you out?'

'No, dear. I climbed up the ladder and asked *him*. He protested at first. "Miss Diana! If His Lordship catches you talking to the likes of me, he'll have me shot." I took no notice, won him round and we stayed up on that roof until the moon came out.'

'So *that's* where you learned to lay the leaf tiles on your hut,' Gemma grinned.

'Yes, actually. By watching him, like you watched your father. Anyway, how's that fish doing?'

The fish was cooked. They sat and ate it with their fingers in the firelight and it was the best fish Gemma had ever tasted, despite all the little bones. She gave the crispy skin to Duke and went to bed.

Monti kept an omnibus edition of *Sherlock Holmes* under her pillow. It was one of the few treasures she'd taken with her from the mansion when her father died, leaving her his entire estate.

'What did you do with all the money?' Gemma asked, sleepily.

'Buried it. Burned it,' said Monti, briskly. 'Better to start a new chapter.'

She picked up the book and read to Gemma out loud. Although technically she was a mother, she'd never had the chance to read to her own child and the experience was bittersweet.

Afterwards, when Holmes had tied up the loose ends of a most intriguing case, Monti tucked the heavy tapestry curtain that served as a blanket around Gemma and said goodnight.

''Night, Monti . . . Monti?'

'Mmm?'

'Do you ever think about your son?'

Monti put the book away.

'Only every day. No more than all parents do.'

She blew out the candles.

In the darkness, in an unknown prison cell, Jim Diamond was thinking about his daughter.

Chapter 9

While Gemma was learning to survive in the wilderness, Jim Diamond was struggling to come to terms with being held in captivity.

The prison cell itself didn't bother him much, even though it had nothing but the most basic human requirements. Some men found these conditions soul destroying, but not Jim. He'd endured cramped spaces and a lack of beautiful things all his life and didn't recognise it as a particular hardship.

Likewise, the prison food. While some of the inmates gagged at the thought of the tasteless gobs of meat and cold clumps of unidentified vegetables, Jim looked forward to mealtimes. They offered a break from monotony and at least he knew he would be fed, which was not something he'd always been able to guarantee at home.

Jim wasn't a great cook. His father had been handy with a can opener and had brought him up on a diet of tinned food, toast and cereal. They were inventive meals, though. By mixing a tin of corned beef with a packet of dried potato, some tomato sauce and a few frozen peas, he would produce a hash second to none.

These recipes were passed onto Jim but when he married, he filed them in a distant part of his brain and for three years, he ate like a king. Each meal his wife made for him was a gastronomic gift of love, and the gifts got bigger and richer and heavier until he longed for something plain and simple.

'A boiled egg would be lovely,' he'd suggest, and she'd smile and say boiled eggs it would be. But she thought he was worthy of more. Boiled egg and toast was an insult to the man she loved so dearly.

When the egg arrived, it had been sliced, arranged on a large bed of pasta, smothered in creamy sauce and sprinkled with grated cheese. Jim poked the rich mess down his gullet as gracefully as he could because he couldn't bear to upset her. Soon, the rigid little blocks of muscle in his belly disappeared under a cushion of fat and his face grew round.

For three short years, life was perfect. He had a wife, a daughter and a father. For someone who'd never experienced a family as a child, it felt like he'd won the star prize. He could never quite believe his luck.

When his father died, he was sad, but not sorry. His father had suffered from a kind of dementia which started a year after Gemma was born. Jim and his wife had given up their bedroom and looked after him in their small flat together.

They comforted each other as Will turned from a gentle, melancholy soul to an angry, rambling old man. He would wander off and say he was going back to France. At night, Jim's wife would read him detective stories to help him sleep and often he would become confused and call her by another woman's name.

Towards the end, he clutched Jim's hand in an agitated way and told him he would inherit a fortune.

When he died, he hadn't even left a will. All Jim had to remember him by was a ring with a small diamond that his father always wore on the little finger of his left hand.

They'd taken that from him in prison. They'd taken everything from him, right down to his shoelaces. He'd befriended one of the warders and begged to be given back his photograph of Gemma. At first, he stuck the photo to the wall of his cell, but after five minutes, he couldn't bear to see her trapped behind bars like that. It was no place for a little girl.

He took the photo down and put her under his pillow, but then he felt she might suffocate. In the end, he tweaked the staples out of a magazine, bent them into a makeshift pin and fixed the photo to the inside of his shirt, next to his chest.

He was convinced she was dead. It seemed to be the pattern of things. First his wife, now Gemma. He found himself starting to think like his father. These people had been too good for the likes of him and they had been taken away. He didn't deserve them.

As the weeks wore on, there was still no news of Gemma. There had been a big police hunt and a blaze of publicity at the beginning but now it seemed she'd been forgotten. She hadn't, of course. The police had simply run out of leads. There were posters in railway stations up and down the country, but Jim didn't know that. All he knew was what he read in the newspaper and there was no longer any mention of his daughter.

That was, until the day before his trial. One of the other prisoners was reading an article in the paper out loud to another inmate. When Jim appeared, the man stopped reading and quickly turned the page, but it was too late. Jim had spotted the headline.

'Missing Girl's Body Discovered in Lake'

He read it again. He broke out into a sweat. His head

spun, he couldn't see.

'Jim... you all right, mate?'

He retched, but his stomach was empty, there was nothing to throw up but awful bile.

'Jim... Jim? Call the screws! He's going to pass out.'

As his legs buckled under him, he felt someone supporting him under the armpits. He couldn't see properly, he tried to call her,

'Gemmaaaaa!... Gemmaaaaaa!'

But he couldn't hear his own scream. The rest of the inmates looked away as two burly warders carted him off to the prison hospital and strapped him down.

Gemma had never felt more alive. She woke at dawn, washed, made the bed and ate a large breakfast of mushrooms. Duke, attracted by the smell of frying fungi had almost burnt his nose on the pan in an attempt to steal one. He'd already gulped down the remains of a fat rabbit he'd stolen from a fox and having enjoyed his meat course, he was looking for a few vegetables to go with it.

Monti was sitting outside on a stool making a length of rope out of grass.

'Make yourself useful, Jimmy Scar!' she called. 'Finish this off for me, will you?'

Gemma went and sat next to her. 'Why do we need more rope?'

Monti looked at her as if she was daft. 'You can never have too much rope. Wicks for lamps, weapons, traps, nets, belts, climbing, halters, hold-ups, hatbands...'

She handed the long skein of grass to Gemma. She took it in her right hand, twisted the left strand two turns, pushed it under the right, then she did the same with the right strand. It was a bit like plaiting hair.

Monti had shown her how to make rope with all the patience of a mother teaching her favourite daughter how to knit. Gemma picked it up easily and now she could do it without looking.

The crushed stems oozed their indelible green ink into her palms. She loved to watch the rope turn from an armful of fuzzy, wild grass into a tamed piece of equipment with its own pattern and purpose.

Gemma watched as Monti plaited her own, moon-white hair into a long braid and trapped it under her hat.

'Where are you going?'

'Tracking.'

She took a pot of wild honey and rubbed it onto her hands.

'Why do you do that? Is it like handcream?'

'It helps to disguise human scent.'

'What if you're superhuman. Does it work then?'

Monti rolled her eyes and offered her the jar.

'Oh . . . can I come?' she asked.

'You're free to go where you please,' said Monti. 'I've told you that.'

Gemma waited to see if Monti would load her gun. She wanted so much to go with her. She wanted to be like Monti – self-sufficient! That way, if there was no one left to care for her, she could care for herself.

'What are you going to track?'

Monti tutted. 'The whole point of tracking is to see what's out there,' she said. 'Could be anything.'

'Will you shoot whatever it is?'

'Maybe not,' she said. 'I might trap it.'

'Isn't that cruel?'

Monti snapped her gun across her knee and fed it with pellets.

'That depends on your view,' she said. 'I only kill what I need to eat. I don't eat much and nothing goes to waste.'

'But don't the animals suffer?'

'I don't let them suffer, Jimmy Scar. The way I do it, they don't even know they've died. Frightened animals don't taste very good.'

'Why?'

'The fear running through them makes the meat tough. Pass me that rope.'

Gemma handed it to her and watched as Monti fed it into one of the panniers in her ballgown coat where it settled like a coiled snake.

'Coming then?'

Gemma nodded. Her hands were shaking slightly. She was anticipating a cross between a treasure hunt and a grisly murder. While the murderous part filled her with the worst kind of dread, the idea of stalking appealed to her no end. Remembering that she was free to do as she pleased, she decided that if she couldn't face the final curtain, she would simply walk away. Or shut her eyes. Or run.

Pacing behind Monti's flowing gown like a nervous bridesmaid, she followed her into the forest. Now and again, she would step on a twig and it would snap crisply, causing Monti to whisk round and glare at her.

'I can't help it!' she mouthed.

Monti took her aside.

'We might as well walk along banging a drum!' she

said. 'The foliage is brittle, every little crackle carries a long distance. *Stalk*, don't walk! Balance on the outside edge of your feet, toe to heel!'

'Sorry, Monti.'

'Accepted...I'll show you how to look for signs. Top, middle and bottom. What you want to do is divide your body into three.'

Gemma looked confused, so Monti demonstrated like an air hostess pointing out the exit doors to passengers on a Jumbo Jet.

'Top signs are from the shoulders up!' she announced. She pointed to the treetops and clapped her hands loudly, causing a flock of birds to clatter nervously into the sky.

'Birds fluttering from branches warn animals below that an enemy is approaching!'

'And we're the enemy?' frowned Gemma.

'Got it.'

Monti drew an invisible line between her shoulder and knee.

'Middle signs!' she said. 'Look for branches pushed aside by large animals, little tufts of hair caught on twigs.' She examined a branch which rested at waist height. 'What do you see?'

Gemma squinted at the bark and noticed a small, raw scar on it. 'Is that something?'

Monti nodded. 'Deer been rubbing against it,' she said. 'Bottom signs!'

Gemma giggled.

'Pay attention!' Monti crouched down. 'I'm looking for tracks, droppings, urine...'

She reminded Gemma very much of Sherlock Holmes.

'Yes, well it's the same, isn't it? We're looking for clues,' said Monti. 'Broken twigs, burrows, spit, fur...'

Gemma joined in the search and found a small, purplish splash. 'Bird poo?'

Monti gave her a withering look.

'*Bird* poo? You'll have to be a bit more specific than that. What sort of bird poo? Game bird? Tree-nester? And who's to say it's not bat poo?'

'I don't know.'

'Did it fall from a great height or was it deposited on the ground, would you say?'

Gemma looked at the splash marks on the nearby leaves and poked the dropping with a small stick. 'A great height? And it's full of pips!'

'So, it's a tree-rooster and it's a berry-eater,' said Monti. 'And there's not much of it, so by process of elimination, I'd say it was probably a finch dropping, my dear Watson!'

Gemma was enjoying this game. She found she was starting to use her eyes in a completely different way. Clues that had previously seemed invisible were now glaringly obvious. She could hardly believe she'd never noticed them before.

She didn't just look straight ahead anymore. She looked down, up, forwards and sideways. Animals tend to look two ways, Monti told her, forwards and down. It was impossible for any creature except a bird to move across the ground without leaving a sign.

After a while, they came across a meadow. Gemma was waist-high in the glossy yellow heads of what seemed to be giant buttercups.

'Listen with your eyes and look with your ears,'

Monti advised. Suddenly, she dropped down and waved Gemma over. Running through the meadow was a thin, trickling stream.

'Hare tracks,' she said, parting the grass to reveal a neat footprint in the softened mud. Gemma peered at it.

'How do you know it's not a rabbit?' she wondered.

'Hares bound, rabbits hop,' Monti replied. 'And hares have got hairy pads on their feet. See how the claw marks are blurred?'

'Oh... yes!' Gemma was impressed.

'That's nothing' said Monti. 'Charlie Coggins could tell just by looking at an animal track whether the animal was male or female. He could tell its weight, its age and its inside leg measurement.'

'How?'

Monti traced the pawmark with her finger.

'Say it was a fit, young hare. The tracks wouldn't be as deep or as long as an older animal's and the clawmarks would be finer. This one stopped for a drink... see where its belly fur has left an impression?'

Gemma looked at the fine, wavy, comb marks and picked out a couple of white fibres.

'Can animals read the tracks too?'

'They're the experts,' said Monti. 'Better than us at using their noses too. An old fox wouldn't waste his energy tracking a feisty little hare when he can smell an old, injured one sitting round the corner.'

'Yes, but how can we tell if the tracks are fresh?'

'Lots of ways,' said Monti. 'For a start, if the tracks are more than two days old, they'll have bits of grass or foliage stuck in the surface.'

'And you learnt all this from Charlie Coggins?'

Gemma wished she'd met him. How nice it would have been to miss boring old school lessons like Monti had done and spend the afternoons learning *useful* things instead.

'Is Charlie still around, Monti?'

Monti screwed up her nose.

'If he is, he's covered his tracks,' she replied. 'He's probably stalking St. Peter by now.'

'You think he went to heaven then, despite him thieving off your father?'

'I have no experience of heaven,' Monti announced. 'But I do know my own father and he was a worse thief than Charlie Coggins ever was. Coggins only took what he needed. Father took what he wanted. There is a big difference, Jimmy Scar.'

Gemma had a question she'd wanted to ask for ages.

'Monti . . . ?'

'Sssshh!'

Monti was listening to something. She cocked her ear like Duke. Silently, she drew her gun out and started to stalk forward, away from the sun. She raised the weapon to her shoulder in the same faultless, fluid manner Jim Diamond employed with his hammer.

Suddenly, a hare sprang out of the buttercups. Gemma saw the moleskin glove squeezing the trigger.

'Did you love your father, Monti?' she blurted.

BANG!

A thousand hidden birds exploded into the cloudless sky as the hare zigzagged across the meadow, leaving a parting in its wake. Monti lowered the gun. She stood with her back towards the cowering girl like a malignant scarecrow.

Gemma, who had picked up quite a few survival techniques by now, decided the best course of action was to hide.

Chapter 10

Summer was over and the schoolchildren had long since settled in their new classes. There had been a special assembly for Gemma where at least two of the girls cried and regretted the cruel remarks they'd made to her.

There had been prayers hoping for her safe return and a reminder never to speak to strangers which prompted everybody to form disturbing pictures of the fate that might have befallen their classmate.

Many couldn't sleep. Many, who had felt quite happy walking to and from school alone, suddenly felt themselves looking over their shoulders or asking their parents to collect them.

Jim Diamond remained in custody. Owing to a paralysis which the prison doctor decided was due to hysterical depression, he had been unfit to stand trial on the due date and it had been postponed.

Despite being told that the body in the lake was that of another child who had drowned after a boating accident, Jim had convinced himself that Gemma was lost forever and no longer cared whether he was found innocent or guilty.

The leaves were turning gold in the forest. Duke had lost all trace of his puppy fat and was growing lean and muscular with a thick, wiry coat. Monti was sure he had wolfhound blood in him.

He had become very close friends with Cecil B. If it was windy or raining, the old mule would stand there, comfortable as an old kitchen table and let Duke shelter under his belly. In return, Duke would snap at the bothersome flies that Cecil couldn't reach and eat them like currants.

One of Gemma's less charming tasks was to gather the large, fibrous balls of dung that exploded out of Cecil B and stack them in a steaming pile to dry. These, she was told, would make excellent winter fuel on days when wood was in short supply.

'Just think of it as recycled hay and nuts,' said Monti as Gemma wrinkled her nose. 'We have to think ahead. Winter will be hard upon us before we know it, Jimmy Scar. Food will be scarce. We must stock up our larder.'

There was much harvesting to be done. There had been a long trip taken under the cover of darkness on the back of Cecil B to scythe corn from a distant field.

They had gathered great, golden armfuls of it, the bulk of which they stuffed into two woven panniers on the mule's back. The rest, they tied in big sheaves around their bodies and travelled home under the milky stars like human corn dollies.

'Don't you ever get lost, Monti?' wondered Gemma, for she never used a compass of any kind and human signposts were non-existent.

'There are signposts everywhere,' said Monti. 'Star signposts, animal signposts. According to the Gospel of Coggins, swallows won't nest facing north, pheasants roost to the south, all plants look to the light.'

'And is it all true?'

'We're home, aren't we?' replied Monti.

And there in the distance was the welcoming glow of a tallow candle.

The next morning, they stripped off the corn ears and ground them down into a greyish flour which would be used for making bread and cakes in the cold months ahead.

Berries and fruit of all description were picked, cleaned and packed. They were turned into jams, jellies and cordials. Wild rosehips were dried off in the mud oven and bottled for syrup which Monti said was a very good source of vitamin C. Elder and juniper berries were steeped in alcohol and left to ferment.

Vegetables, roots and tubers were stored in trays or pickled. Herbs of every description were tied in bunches and hung from canes all around the dwelling, filling the room with the fading perfume of summer.

Some would be ground with a pestle and mortar, twisted in paper and stored in an airtight tin for medicinal purposes. There were blackberry roots to use as astringent, the white ashes of maple leaves to ease fever and tonics made from camomile and willow.

The more fragrant herbs were saved to flavour the cooking or to be mixed into toiletries.

Monti was skinning another rabbit. She did it so swiftly, it was as if she were helping a toddler out of its jumper. She had a pile of pelts ready to cure, all of which had to be rubbed clean with sand, rinsed, hung and beaten until they were supple.

This process was helped swiftly along by a generous sprinkling of urine, hot from the mule. Apparently, Cecil B's contribution contained a lot of natural salts that improved the condition of the leather no end.

Gemma played with the gun idly on her knee. She had learnt to strip it down and load it. She would tuck it into her shoulder and curl her finger around the trigger but she had never once fired a shot.

She didn't want to, but she knew how. Had she tried, she felt she would have been a crack shot. This pleased her, because even if she never killed an animal, she knew she had the skill to defend herself in the unlikelihood of being confronted by Mr Kasheffi.

'Put some green stuff on the fire,' Monti called. 'We need to cure the rest of this meat.'

Gemma put the gun down. She searched outside in the shade for a large fern, tore off a handful of spore-covered fronds and arranged them on the dying fire. The vapour rose in a soft haze. She sprinkled the embers with damp grass until the smoke was rolling gently, then fetched the old, split log Monti always used and pinned strips of meat to it.

There was no wind to speak of, so once the plank was in position, the smoke penetrated the meat evenly, sealing in the juices and forming a light crust. Preserved like this, they would be able to eat it on Christmas Day.

It was the glowing embers that made Gemma suddenly think of Christmas. Christmas had always been tinged with an intangible sadness, even though she and her father would never admit it to each other. They would go to great lengths to decorate a plastic tree and he would get behind with his bills in order to buy something he thought she'd really like.

They would make each other cards, there would be a small frozen turkey, crackers and paper hats and they would wish each other such a merry Christmas but secretly, they always suspected that families with both parents were having a better one.

Gemma didn't want to think about Christmas. Not now. She was happy for now, in the forest, with the bees crash-landing in the freaky, breathless heat and the air over-ripe with sweating fruit. But the thought kept coming back. She might have to spend Christmas without her father.

'Do you think he'll be looking for me?' she asked Monti that night. 'Do you think he might be out of prison and wondering where I am?'

'He could be. Where would he go if he was out of prison?'

Gemma was going to say, 'To our new place near the park.' Then she realised the new flat would have been let to someone else long ago.

'I don't know. I wish you got a newspaper!' she snapped. 'There might have been something in it about him.'

Monti glared at her.

'Newspaper! *Newspaper*? If you want the truth about something, you don't buy a newspaper! I haven't read one in forty years. Not after the damned lies they told about me.'

Gemma had never seen her look so angry.

'They called my son *filthy* names!' she said. 'My son, three months old and they called him filthy names because I didn't marry the father! Oh, and they said when I was dead, he would inherit the lot and what a scandal it would be, a *peasant* lording it over the gentry. Well, he won't inherit a penny!' she yelled. 'I'd rather he grew up on breadcrusts and dripping like his father than became a rich, bigoted pig like mine!'

Duke slunk into a corner and knocked over the tray of wild seeds that Monti had spent ages sorting into piles. She turned and barked at him.

'Stupid dog! There is not enough room here anymore!'

Gemma, who had been feeling very sorry for Monti up until that point, suddenly flew into a rage which knocked Monti's into a cocked hat.

'Don't you call my dog horrible names!' she yelled. 'You didn't like it when people called your precious son names!'

'You leave my son out of this,' warned Monti. 'You haven't a clue what I have gone through as a mother.'

'Ha!' said Gemma. 'You're the one who doesn't have a clue. You go on and on about how you hate money, but you *chose* to be poor, Monti! You're playing a game! Poor people can't choose to be rich, can they?'

'Good,' said Monti, coldly. 'The more poor people, the better. They are a much nicer breed. Money is evil, Jimmy Scar. Think of my father, think of your Mr Kasheffi!'

'*No* money is worse!' shouted Gemma. 'Think of my father, think of your son!'

Monti tottered backwards, clutching her brooch.

'Get out!' she pointed feebly at the door, her voice wavering. 'Get out!'

'Don't worry, I'm going!' scowled Gemma.

She whistled to Duke out of the corner of her mouth, grabbed her hat and marched into the night.

*

At first, Gemma ran blindly, barefoot through the trees, fearless with rage. A glorious illusion had been shattered. Monti hadn't just been her surrogate mother, she was a goddess. A white witch. All powerful, all holy!

Now? She was just a spoilt, batty old hermit who knew nothing of the modern world and had no friends to speak of except for a smelly old mule.

After a while, she came to a clearing and the stitch in her side forced her to stop. She bent double and tried to fill her lungs with great gulps of oxygen, but there didn't seem to be any. Feeling dizzy, she flopped down and put her head between her knees.

Duke took this as his cue to leap over her, backwards and forwards like a small horse. It was such a ridiculous thing to do and he was taking himself so seriously, she began to laugh. The more she laughed, the higher he jumped.

How silly and small we must seem to the moon! she thought. How silly and small we all are!

She lay back in the damp grass and stared up at the sky. What if the moon started questioning its position in life? What if it went completely against its nature and tried to compete with the sun? The world would go mad!

'Hey, diddle diddle, the cat and the fiddle, the cow jumped over the moon . . . ' Gemma lifted Duke's ear and sang into it, softly: 'The little dog laughed to see such fun – hey, you could have been a cloud . . . or a mule!'

He looked at her, rolled his round, brown eyes towards the stars and howled. She put her arm round him. She could feel his heart pumping and the funny thrusting of his head as he puckered up his hairy lips.

'It's no use howling,' she said. 'The dish ran away

with the spoon. It was their choice. I wonder what the consequences were?'

Somewhere below in the valley, a vixen answered. Once, twice... Duke stopped mid-howl and started to growl softly. He followed this with a series of sharp, determined barks punctuated with a low, dry cough.

'Who are you talking to?' asked Gemma. 'Friend or foe?'

Of course, he couldn't say. Had he been able to, he might have told her he was having a conversation with a poacher's whistle and that the person blowing it had never been less than twenty metres away.

Gemma remembered the rules of survival and had found herself a shelter to spend the night in. It was a small cave made by the root formation of a hollow oak which looked as if it had lifted itself up on gigantic, gnarled toes.

She lined the floor with dry leaves, plugged the entrance with branches and curled up, using Duke as a hotwater bottle.

She was gazing sleepily at the furrowed, wooden walls of her temporary bedroom when an idea sprang into her head. She could build a home in the forest big enough for her father!

The thought made her sit up and bash her closed fist into her palm with excitement. Of course! Why hadn't she thought of it before? It was the answer to everything. They could all live in it together and there would be no nasty landlord, no policemen, no bills, no school!

She would build this home according to her own plans. It would be different from Monti's. Monti's had design faults. It was inclined to be damp. Although she'd waterproofed the animal skin walls with beeswax, the natural shrinking and expanding of the branch frame caused the walls to gape sometimes. In winter, that would cause a howling draught.

She started to design this folly in her head. It was going to have a clay roof. She would dig clay out of the river bed and mould it into tiles. She wondered if it might even be possible to make individual bricks. The prospect of making enough bricks for all four walls was daunting, but surely she could make enough to lay a few courses on top of the foundation?

'A good foundation is everything!' she told herself. It was a phrase Jim often used. She would dig the foundations, then she would lay down a a mixture of pebbles, sand, water and mud to form a solid base and build a low wall upon that. The uprights would be made from hardwood which she would paint with an emulsion prepared from what? Nut oil and egg yolks!

'It will be fantastic, Duke!' she said. 'It's going to have a proper chimney and a fireplace and you will be able to lie in front of it on Christmas Day!'

Of course, the whole project was doomed from the start if she didn't patch things up with Monti, because she needed to borrow her spade. Not to mention a hammer, a saw and a ladder.

'Being as she's not talking to me, I shall just have to borrow them when she's not looking,' she told Duke.

It was going to be difficult, because Monti had eyes everywhere. She would notice her tools missing and track them down, using every trick in Coggins' Bible. She would look for fibres of the thief's hair, nervous footprints left in the dust, a blazing trail of flattened grass, snapped twigs and brambles pushed aside.

Theft was out of the question. She was going to have to tell her about the new house and ask nicely. But what if Monti wouldn't listen?

She drifted off to sleep in the early hours of the morning, planning what to say and wondering whether or not it was best to apologise. Although she meant every word she said during their argument, now she'd had a chance to cool off, she decided maybe they were both in the wrong.

'I'm sorry, Monti. I don't blame you for hating money. I don't want to be rich, I just meant it's awful trying to manage without enough.'

But then Monti would say, 'But it's *never* enough, Jimmy Scar. My father had more than enough and he still wanted more!' and then Gemma would get angry again and say,

'Yes, but if my father had had a little bit more, we wouldn't be in the mess we are today!' Maybe it was best just to tell her she was moving out at Monti's request and given that she would otherwise be homeless, could she please borrow some tools to build her own place?

Monti beat Gemma home the next morning by thirty minutes – just enough time to create the illusion that she'd stayed indoors all night and had just woken up.

Gemma, who usually came and went as she pleased, thought it would be polite to knock on the front door.

'Don't be ridiculous,' Monti called. 'Come in.'

Gemma shuffled inside, expecting to be bawled at like a teenager who had gone to an all-night party and forgotten to tell her parents.

'I have something to say,' said Monti, solemnly.

'What?'

'Not to you, Jimmy Scar, to Duke!'

She held out her hand towards the dog, who obediently pottered up to her, sniffed her fingers and sat down expectantly, his tail thumping.

'I am sorry for calling you a nasty name,' she said. 'It was rude of me. You are a fine, intelligent dog.'

She reached into one of her coat panniers and produced a pheasant and watercress sausage.

'Please accept my apologies,' she said.

Duke accepted them hungrily and ran out into the clearing to show his prize to Cecil B.

Gemma, was touched by Monti's apology, but for some reason, it made her laugh. She covered her mouth with her hand.

'Sorry, Monti. I'm not laughing at you.'

'Well, maybe you should,' said Monti. 'I can be very blinkered, sometimes. I have tried to fight it. Goodness knows it's caused enough heartache, but sometimes, something touches a raw nerve.'

There was a loud, jealous snort from outside as Cecil B got wind of the sausage. Monti grinned broadly. 'I think that may be why I get on so famously with that mule!'

Gemma flung her arms around her. How was it possible to hate someone one minute and love them so utterly the next?

'You are bending my fishhooks,' said Monti.

She wasn't comfortable with such physical demonstrations. Despite her delight that Gemma had come home, she hadn't been held affectionately for many,

many years and it made her feel nervous.

Over breakfast, Gemma mentioned her plans to Monti.

'I was thinking of building my own place.'

She watched Monti's face to see if she could detect any flicker of emotion, but Monti was an accomplished actress.

'Oh?'

'Yes. You see, I think you're right about there not being enough room here and I want to build one for me and my dad.'

Monty nodded her head. 'I see. How will he know where to find you?'

In a flurry of enthusiasm, Gemma explained she would use the money she'd thrown in the bushes to get to the nearest town. Then, she would find a phonebox and ring round all the prisons to find out where her father was. Having found him, she would write a letter telling him about the house and when he was let out of prison, he could come and live there.

'It's a wonderful dream,' said Monty.

'Oh, it's not a *dream*,' said Gemma. 'It's going to be for real, Monti. I'm going to make it happen!'

Chapter 11

Gemma leant the spade against a rock and arched her back. She'd been digging hard all morning, yet she'd hardly made a dent in the foundations she was supposed to be excavating.

She'd marked out the plot carefully with grass rope. She'd chosen the location away from the river so they wouldn't be bothered by insect bites or flooding. At some point, she would dig a well which would be fed by an underground stream.

That was the grand plan; the reality was rather different. The site she'd chosen upon which to build her dreams was so thick with tree roots, it was impossible to dig without mechanical equipment.

She was going to have to think again. It was infuriating, because it was a lovely spot and she'd wasted all that time marking it out. Now the light was beginning to fade. It had been a bright, clean morning with a light breeze wobbling the silver beads on the spiders' webs, but now the sky was a mass of grey bruises.

Gemma felt the energy evaporating through her skin. It would have been nice to stop, to go back to Monti's and lie down for a while but she wanted to push on. She pulled the first wooden peg out of the rope boundary and rolled it up wearily.

It was good of Monti to lend her the spade. She wondered if she would miss her at all when she moved out.

'You can come and visit us whenever you like,' she'd told her.

'Thank you, Jimmy Scar.'

Monti hadn't offered to help build the house beyond lending her the tools and Gemma was grateful for her lack of intrusion. This was her gift to her father. Her way of saying sorry for what she believed she had put him through.

It wouldn't stop at a roof and four walls either. No, that was just the house bit! She was going to make it into a real home with his own, handmade shaving soap waiting for him in a special stone dish and flowers in every room.

She kicked over the traces of the foundations and slung the rope over her arm. Duke was restless. Something was bothering him.

'What's up, Duke? Hungry again? Why don't you catch yourself a rabbit?'

But Duke was too distracted to go hunting.

'Come on, let's find another place to build our palace.'

Gemma swung the spade over her shoulder and headed towards the hill.

Monti had a headache over one eye. She had been brooding indoors, but the atmosphere was suffocating and she was forced to go outside.

She could feel the electricity in the air. Cecil B could too. He was uneasy. A layer of sweat had formed on his flanks and his ears were twitching. He kept lifting his feet as if the vibrations under the earth were tickling his hooves. Monti smoothed the stiff hairs on the ridge of his back.

'Steady, darling. You hear it already, don't you?'

His ears swivelled, cupping and swirling the low rumbles of thunder inaudible to human ears.

'The devil's brewing,' said Monti. 'It's a hellish sky.'

She went indoors, put on her hat and fetched Cecil's bridle from its hook on the low ceiling.

She grabbed a handful of shelled hazelnuts and approached the mule, clicking her tongue.

While he munched, she slipped the bit in his mouth, stood on a log and sprang lightly onto his back. Cecil promptly sat down.

'Cecil, stand!' she commanded. The mule spat out a hazelnut lazily and snorted.

'All right,' said Monti. 'Have it your own way. Cecil, sit!'

From several miles away, there was a muffled boom, as if a small bomb had been dropped. The mule leapt to its feet and turned in a mad circle.

'Thank you.'

Monti steadied his head, tapped him lightly in the ribs and pointed him towards the storm.

'Come on, Duke. It's not much further!' said Gemma. He was in a very strange mood, she decided. He was very reluctant to climb the hill and she had to keep stopping and urging him on.

'Come along! What's the matter? Don't you want a new home with your own willow bed? I'll make you a rabbit fur cushion.'

Duke sniffed the air and whimpered.

'Now you're being silly,' she said. 'It's not as if you'll never see Cecil B again. We'll be neighbours.'

A large drop of water splashed onto her cheek. She held out her hand to catch another one.

'Good!' she said. 'I hope it rains really hard. It will soften the ground and it will be much easier for me to dig.'

She had no idea what geography lay beyond the hill. She was hoping for a small clearing surrounded by shrubs and trees too dense for ramblers to stumble across and beyond that, tall evergreens that would shield her palace from prying aeroplanes.

It was raining heavily now. The hill became greasy underfoot. Gemma slid onto her knees, and had to use the nails of one hand to claw her way up again.

'Oh, Duke! What are you scared of?' she laughed. 'It's only a shower!'

There was a carnivorous roar of thunder and he sank into the grass as if he was being hunted.

She was almost at the top of the hill now. She had her back to Duke and couldn't hear him barking under the thunderclaps. Cecil B galloped into view.

Monti was shouting, but her words were drowned by a climatic drumroll. There was a momentary lull.

'Jimmy Scar!'

Gemma turned, surprised to see her.

'Monti?'

'Give me the spade now!'

Gemma was confused. What was Monti doing here, looking so angry? 'Why do you want it?'

Why had she changed her mind about lending her the spade? Maybe she didn't want her to build the house. That's it, she was jealous. She didn't want her to leave.

Monti had climbed down from the mule and was waving her arms.

'Give me the *spade*!' she mouthed.

Gemma frowned. Monti was clambering up the hill, battling against the rain. She was going to wrench the spade from her! Gemma drew back.

'Why?'

She snatched the spade away from Monti and waved the gleaming tool in the air. If she wanted it that badly, she could come and get it. Silly old woman, trying to destroy her dream!

She ran uphill backwards. Monti ran her down, grabbed the spade handle and pushed the girl as hard as she could. As Gemma fell and rolled helplessly down the hill, the sky split in two and a blinding fork of lightning struck the metal spade.

Monti jerked like a puppet and collapsed, smoke pouring from the remains of her hat.

Her boots had burst and most of her coat had burnt away. There was a sickening smell of burnt hair.

'Monti? Oh, no! . . . *Monti*?'

Gemma dropped to her knees. She tried to find a pulse with her muddy fingers. She could feel something but was that feathery bump, bump just the sound of her own blood pounding through her shaking thumbs?

She looked around anxiously in the thin hope that someone would appear. Someone, anyone who could help.

'I'm only ten,' she sobbed. 'Mummy, help! I don't know what to *do*!'

If an answer came, Duke never heard it. There again, maybe it did come and it was the wrong pitch for a dog to hear, for Gemma rapidly regained her senses.

With an incredible spurt of adrenalin, she lifted Monti up. She draped her over the mule, mounted and drove him down the hill and back through the forest at such speed his feet barely clipped the grass.

She willed the mule onwards through gritted teeth. 'Come on, Cecil B! Come on!'

Duke followed in their wake, stunned by the sudden grace and sheer power that his clompy old friend had managed to muster. Maybe it was Cecil's mother who had answered Gemma's prayers and not her own, for now he was all racehorse, all trace of paternal donkeyness had vanished.

Past the dwelling and nearing the edge of the forest, Gemma found herself slowing the mule down to a trot. There was a huge dilemma. Monti was dying. If Gemma went to find help, she risked being recognised. If she was, things could go two ways. Either she would be reunited with her father. Or she would be taken into care.

She was afraid it would be the latter. What was she to do? Risk her own freedom and save Monti's life or...?

She had no choice. If it hadn't been for this wonderful bundle of wet rags, hooks and hatpins, Gemma would have been struck dead.

A quarter of a mile in from the edge of the forest, there was a small, natural lake.

Stuck in the bank, was a gigantic, green umbrella angled against the rain. On closer inspection, Gemma noticed a pair of large, green wellingtons sticking out and urged Cecil forward.

A man was baiting his fishing hook. Cecil snorted loudly and the man whipped round, stabbing his finger as he did so.

He stared in disbelief at the spectacle before him – a

wild, rain-drenched child astride a mule, over which flopped the ghostly form of something not quite human, the head of which was being guarded by a wolf. He twisted his head to try and make sense of what he was seeing.

'Please help! She's been struck by lightning.'

Gemma's voice brought him back to his senses.

'Oh, Lord . . .' he said. 'Yes, yes of course! My phone . . . I know it's here somewhere.'

He rattled round in a rucksack, pulled out his mobile and jabbed at it urgently. Someone answered and he garbled into the mouthpiece, turning to Gemma for some answers.

'Is she alive?'

Gemma shrugged. The man shook his head at her seeming indifference.

'We don't know,' he told the phone. He explained his whereabouts and switched the phone off.

'They're sending a helicopter.'

Gemma was shivering. He took off his waterproof jacket and put it round her shoulders.

'What are you *doing* out in this weather?' he said. 'Is this . . . she . . . your grandmother?'

Gemma wouldn't answer. She wasn't going to tell anybody anything.

'What's your name?'

The man was staring at her as if he was trying to remember where he'd seen her before. Gemma hid her face in Cecil's mane. He couldn't place her.

'Whatsyourname? Did you try mouth to mouth? Heart massage? Look, I think we should try *something*!'

He didn't know what. His only experience of first aid was what he'd seen on the television.

'Come down from the horse or whatever it is,' he said. 'At least help me wrap her in a rug.' He held a rolled-up tartan blanket to his chest. Gemma stayed where she was.

He was begining to wonder if she was simple in the head. She gazed at him dully, huddled under his coat. In truth, she was so mentally tired, so physically exhausted she didn't have the energy to answer him, even if she'd wanted to. She was unused to riding and seemed to have become painfully welded to Cecil's bare back.

The man held out his hand, but she wouldn't take it. He was afraid to touch her in case she wasn't entirely tame, afraid she might lash out with a claw like a cornered animal. He was also wary of the dog which he felt might snap his hand off if he came closer.

He turned his attention to Monti. The stench of smoke and the possibility that she was dead revolted him, but he felt if he wrapped her up, the spectacle would be less awful.

Inching towards her, bracing himself to be attacked by Duke, he slid his hands under her body, scared she would turn to ash in his arms.

Duke backed away under Cecil and watched quietly. The man supported Monti on his forearms. She was surprisingly light under the burden of her wet, tattered shroud. As he lifted her off the mule, pins, knives, hooks and clips spilled from her like an open jewellery box.

He spread the rug out with his foot and laid her down. Now that he could see her face, despite the burns, he was struck by how handsome she was. Regal, in fact. He imagined how she might once have looked like the dark, brooding child staring down at him.

The metal part of Monti's diamond brooch had

melted. He held it aside and put his ear to her chest. There was the faintest tick.

'There's something!' he murmured to himself. He was wondering what to do for the best. If he massaged her heart the wrong way, might it kill her?

Mouth to mouth, then! He knew he had to tip the head back and clear the airway and was very conscious that he had last had his hand in a pot of maggots. Did it matter? It bothered him terribly. He should clean his hands in the lake.

Just as he was dithering, Duke began to bark. He'd heard the whirr of the helicopter long before it appeared through the clouds, droning towards them like a mechanical dragonfly.

The man stood up and waved his arms.

'Hi! Over *here*! . . . Over *here*!'

It landed about fifty metres away, shattering the peace of the forest and creating a sinister whirlwind.

Two men and a woman in overalls climbed out and ran towards them with medical bags and a stretcher. They knelt over Monti, pulling equipment out of one of the bags. Someone was lifting Gemma off the mule.

'Come on, love. I've got you. Down you come. What's your name?'

She was being wrapped in a blanket. She couldn't move her arms. They were firing questions at her.

'Can you tell us your name, pet?'

'Who's the lady?'

'Where did it happen. Can you remember?'

She couldn't see what they were doing to Monti. Gemma tried to fight them off. 'Get off me. I want to stay with her!'

She tried to run to Monti, but they held onto her tightly, trying to calm her down.

'Don't worry. You can be with her soon.'

They bundled her towards the helicopter.

'Duke!' she cried. 'What about Duke?'

'That man will hang onto him,' they reassured her. 'Can you look after the dog and the donkey, sir? Just until the police arrive.'

They pushed Gemma's head down to protect her from the great, whipping blades.

'Duke, come!' she screamed, but her voice was drowned out.

'**Duuuuke!**'

She watched him out of the helicopter window, growing smaller and smaller until he looked like a toy dog with a little, plastic mule. He was jumping up in the air, higher and higher, trying to grab the helicopter in his jaws like a stick and bring it back down to earth.

Then he disappeared beneath the clouds.

Chapter 12

The prison warder rattled his keys in Jim's cell door.

'Look lively, Diamond,' he said. 'Gov'nor wants to see you.'

Jim opened his eyes, his head was still fuzzy with sedatives.

'What's he want?'

'Get your shoes on and you'll find out.'

Jim swung his legs slowly off the bed. He tried to think why he was being summoned, but right now, he couldn't manage to think and put his shoes on at the same time. He stared at his feet for a while, not entirely sure they were his and groped for his prison-issue shoes. He found them under the bed and arranged them on the floor in front of him.

'Come on, man. Put them on.'

The shoes were far too large. They forced him to walk like a clown.

'Are these my shoes?'

The warder looked at them, then at his watch.

'Come on, Coco, I'll race you there,' he said.

Jim slopped along behind his keeper, grabbing at the walls to steady himself. His legs felt so rubbery, he could hardly stand. The warder, who was not an unkind man, put out his hand to steady him.

'Whoops, had a pint of lager, have we?' he quipped.

Jim looked at him blankly. Was it some sort of joke

about the lager? A constant, metallic clanging filled his head. It was inescapable. Day in, day out, asleep or awake it was there, this nerve-shattering dropping of tin trays onto hard floors. If he put his fingers in his ears, it got worse, as if the noise was coming from inside him. Maybe it was. Maybe the prison was a silent place and he was imagining the noise.

He bumbled down the corridor and almost bumped into the warder who had stopped sharply and was knocking on a door.

'Come in.'

'Prisoner 87479, sir.' The warder steered Jim into the room.

The Governor looked up from his notes and smiled at him.

'How are you feeling?'

Jim thought about it. The Governor waited patiently.

'Would you like a chair?'

Jim nodded, but didn't sit down. He blinked at the Governor slowly, half-wondering if he'd committed another crime for which he was about to be punished. He couldn't remember having done anything, but that was no guarantee.

'I've got some very good news for you, Diamond. Your daughter is alive.'

Jim put his head on one side, as if the Governor had spoken to him in a foreign language and he was trying to guess the content of the message by the tone of his voice.

'Did you hear what I said?'

Jim mouthed the words, aware of the exaggerated shape of his lips, the movement of his tongue as he pronounced them.

'My . . . daughter . . . is . . . alive.'

'Yes, she was found yesterday by a fisherman who alerted the emergency services.'

Jim felt a rush of blood flushing the drugs from the part of his brain he needed to use. He was suddenly alert, wide eyed!

'My daughter is alive?'

He was grinning like an idiot. The Governor shuffled the papers around his desk, unable for his own personal reasons to look at the prisoner before him.

'Yes, it's excellent news. She will be cared for temporarily in a children's home until your release or until such times as social services decide . . . '

'My daughter is alive?'

The Governor trailed off and put his glasses on.

'I have a new trial date for you which is . . . let me see now . . . '

There was a dull thump, as if someone had dropped a sack of potatoes. The Governor peered over his spectacles to discover Prisoner 87479 slumped on the carpet in a dead faint.

He had fallen right out of his shoes.

'I want to see my father, let me out!' shouted Gemma, hammering at the door with her fist. 'You let me *out*!'

The manageress of Park View Children's Home rolled her eyes. It had been a long day and Gemma had been nothing but trouble since she arrived.

She had already tried to escape from hospital after the doctor had checked her over. Although she had insisted her name was Jimmy Scar, the pilot who flew the rescue helicopter suspected who she was and one of the porters also mentioned her likeness to the missing Diamond girl.

As soon as Gemma saw a policewoman walking towards her, she ran out of the examination room and skidded off down the corridor. She was eventually recaptured getting out of a lift on the ground floor and taken to a small room. A social worker was summoned. If she would just say who she was, where she'd been and who the old lady was, she could see her father.

Desperate to see him but not knowing whether Monti would live or die, she spat out her real name.

'I'm Gemma Diamond, okay?'

Apart from that, she refused to answer any questions. She left the hospital in a taxi with the social worker, thinking they were going to the prison, but they weren't. She was being taken to the Children's Home. The woman had lied to her. She'd said she could see her father!

Twice she tried to escape through the window. She needed to go and see Monti. If Monti was still alive, she wanted to let her know she'd be there for her. She'd get her out of the hospital and take her back to the forest.

Now Gemma had been moved to a room on the ground floor and the windows had been locked.

'You have to calm down,' called the manageress. 'Gemma, if you calm down, you can come into the recreation area and play table tennis with the others.'

'I want to see my father. Unlock the door. You're not *allowed* to lock the door!'

There was no reply. Whether the door was locked or the manageress was just holding it shut, she didn't know. She waited on the bed for a minute then tried the door again. It opened. The woman was still standing there with her arms folded. She came into the room.

'Let's talk,' she said.

'I don't *want* to talk!'

Gemma threw herself back onto the bed and hid her face in the pillow. She felt the bed lower as the woman sat down beside her.

'You will be able to see your father,' she said. 'But you must wait for a visiting order.'

'Why? I'm not a visitor! Why do I have to wait to see my own dad?'

The manageress examined the locks on the windows. The screws were worked loose from their fittings.

'Gemma, if you hadn't run away on your first day here, you could have visited him then. Arrangements had been made but you blew it. Now I'm afraid you'll have to wait.'

'I won't!'

The woman stood up.

'Have you been trying to undo these window locks?'

Gemma looked away.

'If you try and escape again, there won't be a visit at all,' she said. 'It's up to you.'

She walked out, leaving the door ajar.

'I'll leave it open,' she called. 'I'm trusting you, okay?'

Gemma took the nail file out of her trouser pocket. She didn't like the trousers. They were too tight. She felt trapped. She wanted her bleached, cut-off shorts back, but they said they weren't fit to wear and gave her a plastic bag full of secondhand stuff. It smelled of charity shops.

She inserted the nail file into one of the screws on the window lock. This morning, she'd had every intention of running to the prison to see her father. She hadn't realised there had to be a special piece of paper. All right then, she'd go to the hospital. They'd taken Monti to intensive care. It couldn't be that hard to find the right ward.

Gemma twiddled the screw out of its hole. It was just like the ones she'd used to fix the door to Duchess's kennel. 'Doors,' she said out loud. 'They keep you in or they keep you out.'

She'd been talking to herself a lot in Park View. Monti used to do it back at the dwelling, she recalled. She often gave a running commentary on what she was doing or asked herself questions out loud. She said it was to do with being alone for so long.

What if the unthinkable happened and Monti died? It raised so many worrying questions. Could Cecil B fend for himself? Did he need the deerskin blanket Monti always gave him in the winter or not? She didn't know.

How long would the dwelling survive without constant repair and attention? How long before the wind and rain stripped the wax from the skin walls and they became pulpy and rotten? How long before horsetails thrust their prehistoric, green heads through the unswept gaps of the stone floor and filled the room?

If Monti died, would she ever get to build the house for her father in time for Christmas? She tried to picture the cards on the mantelpiece, one from Dad, one from her, one from Monti. Moving down, she imagined the glow of the flames dancing in the grate and stretched out on the rug, would be Duke.

Only he wasn't there, was he? She missed him so much.

Gemma put the screw back in the window lock and tightened it so hard, the nail file bent and she took a tiny layer of skin off her finger.

No Dad, no Monti, no Duke.

She closed the door quietly and got into bed. There was nothing to escape for.

Monti opened one eye to make sure there were no nurses about. She pushed back the bedcover and tiptoed down the ward, limping slightly in her hospital gown. She was carrying a green plastic bag which she'd stolen from a patient who was supposed to be going home that afternoon.

In it was a maroon jumper, a pair of gentleman's brown, wool trousers, a tweed jacket, a pair of slip-on shoes, some boxer shorts, a tweed cap, a belt and a packet of glacier mints.

Monti looked over her shoulder and slipped into the ladies' toilets. Ten minutes later, she emerged, disguised in the clothes. Making sure that the coast was clear, she headed out of the ward, down the fire escape and into the car park.

She hadn't seen a car in years and couldn't believe how many there were, and how very small they seemed compared to her father's Rolls-Royce.

There were people everywhere. She could hardly tell which were men and which were woman. They all seemed to be dressed alike. She'd noticed that in the ward when the other patients had visitors. None of the women wore gloves or hats or elegant shoes anymore. They all wore those rubber lace-up gym shoes like Jimmy Scar.

Lying in her narrow hospital bed, she had been annoyed that Jimmy Scar hadn't visited her and assumed she must be in the forest, busy building her folly.

She couldn't remember a thing about the accident, the lifesaving mule-dash or the helicopter trip. All she knew was that she'd been struck by lightning and was lucky to be alive.

She'd asked the nurses if a Jimmy Scar had been asking for her at all, but no one had heard of him, of course.

She had been in intensive care for three days and then amazed them all by suddenly snapping out of her coma and demanding to get out of bed. Technically, the consultant said, she should be dead. At the very least, she should have suffered brain damage.

By the second week, she was ranting and raving so much, the long-suffering nurses suspected she wasn't right in the head and she had another scan, which proved negative. A psychiatrist was brought in who specialised in geriatrics and further tests were conducted. He concluded that while she was cantankerous and certainly eccentric, it was just her personality. The lightning strike was in no way to blame.

Apart from her burns which were healing nicely, there didn't seem to be a great deal wrong with her and it was decided she was fit enough to receive a visit from the police very shortly 'to tie up a few ends' about a missing child.

Worried she might accidentally say something that would lead them to Jimmy Scar, Monti decided to escape.

Although she didn't even know which town she was

in, she had the homing instinct of a carrier pigeon and knew to take a left at the car park exit. Having got to the busy high street, she fortified herself with a glacier mint and decided to look for a tram.

Of course, there were none. They had been replaced by buses years ago. Monti had never been on a bus. She soon realised that in order to catch one, she would have to stand in a queue behind a loud group of boys with red and green spiky hair.

They poked each other in the ribs, then one of them spoke to her.

'All right, Grandad?'

She nodded and smiled. Just then, the bus pulled up. She turned to one of the punks.

'Where does this ...this motorised vehicle go to, boy?'

'It says on the *front*, look! Lost yer glasses, you poor old fing?'

Monti found herself swept onto the bus by the crowd. Everyone who got on flashed a card at the driver or gave him money for a ticket. It was Monti's turn. The driver drummed the ticket machine and waited as she stood there, penniless.

'Where's your bus-pass, mate?'

'My bus-pass?'

The driver rolled his eyes.

'Try looking in your pocket,' he suggested.

Monti pretended to search.

'I think I left it in my other trousers,' she said. By now, the people behind her were getting impatient.

'What's the hold-up?'

'Hurry up. I ain't got all day, you know.'

The driver waved Monti on.

'Go on, you silly old twit. Next time *remember* it, will you?'

'Probably does it all the time,' said the woman behind her. 'Probably loaded.'

Monti watched out of the window as the bus wheezed up the hill. It stopped and started so many times, she started to feel slightly sick.

Everything was so dirty. Everyone was so bad-tempered and graceless and in a hurry. The only people with any charm were the women in saris.

She looked in the green bag. Right at the bottom, wrapped in hospital toilet tissue was her brooch. The nurse told her the rest of her clothes and possessions had been destroyed, but they had saved the brooch. They were going to put it in a safety deposit box for her, but she insisted the diamonds were only paste, so they'd let her keep it in the locker by her bed.

She fingered the melted filigree round the edge. She was worried the lightning might have soldered the little catch at the back behind the pin, but to her relief, it hadn't. It was just a bit stiff. She fidgeted with the catch until the back popped open and looked at the photograph of the baby boy inside.

'Home, James,' she whispered.

Duke was tired of waiting. Having given the fisherman the slip as soon as the helicopter was out of sight, he'd run back to the forest with Cecil B and waited patiently for Gemma to return.

Later that evening, there was still no sign of her, so he decided to go hunting. She would, he was sure, be back soon.

Having caught himself a small shrew and little else, he wandered back to base to see if there was anything roasting over the fire.

But no one was home. Cecil B, who had grown used to a handful of nuts around this time of the evening was in a particularly foul mood. He was doubly annoyed that nobody was there to take his bridle off and refused point blank to let Duke stand under him.

Duke, in return, decided to nip Cecil's ankle and was rewarded with a swift kick.

The next day, they still weren't talking. Cecil had wandered off on his own to find some sustaining thistles and Duke felt lonely.

He sniffed Gemma's bed. The human scent was starting to fade, raising alarm bells in his canine mind.

He stuck it out for two weeks. Then, when her perfume had almost vanished, he carried the last molecules of scent in the lining of his nose and went to look for her.

Chapter 13

The bus sneezed to a halt and the engine stopped. Monti was the only passenger left, sitting right at the back. The driver got out of his cab and tapped on the window.

'End of the line, mate.'

'Pardon?'

'This is the bus depot. I'm clocking off.'

He opened the automatic doors and waited for Monti to get off. She hobbled down the aisle in her tweed cap and gentleman's trousers and refused to let him help her down the steps.

'There's nothing wrong with me!' she snapped. 'Where am I?'

'Cloud Cuckoo Land,' he said.

Monti sniffed the air and detected the lightest whiff of open countryside above the thick stink of diesel fuel. She turned right and followed her nose.

After an hour of walking, she left the town traffic behind her and came to a small village. There was a post office and a greengrocer's with all sorts of fruit and vegetables displayed in pyramids on an artificial grass cloth.

The smell was intoxicating after the dreadful hospital food and Monti couldn't resist.

When no one was looking, she took an apple, an orange, and a large carrot and slipped them into her bag. Then she picked up a bunch of seedless grapes, secreted them under her cap and decided to cut through the churchyard.

She sat down on a bench, ate the grapes and read some of the epitaphs on the gravestones. It suddenly dawned on her that the only man she'd ever loved could be dead by now. If not, he'd be even older than she was. She tried to imagine him bald, bent and toothless, but it was impossible.

She had preserved him in her mind like the fruit in her jam. He would always remain fresh and sweet. If she met him again, he would still be a young man with clear, green eyes and a shock of black, floppy hair oiled into a quiff. How shocked he would be if he saw her now! She was certain he would find her ugly and she felt ashamed.

Monti finished the fruit and went on her way, scolding herself for dwelling on the past. She was lucky she had a future at all and offered a quick prayer of thanks to whoever might be listening, in case she was struck by a thunderbolt to add to her injuries.

On the end of the village she found a footpath which led around the edge of a wheatfield. The wheat had already been harvested and the field ploughed into cabbage-sized clumps of earth.

There was a sign halfway down the footpath by a wooden stile. It said: 'Wheatfield's Riding School ¼ mile'. Monti had guessed as much without having to read the words. She had already read the ground and noted a small pile of rabbit pellets flattened by the unmistakable arc of a horseshoe.

It could have been any old horse of course, but by applying the Laws of Coggins, she noted the depth and angle of the imprint and decided it belonged to a sluggish pony weighed down by a novice rider who weighed around three stone. The flattened grass at the side had also been trampled by small but heavy boots, indicating the horse was being led by a stout person, probably female.

Putting those facts together, it wasn't difficult to conclude that this was a horse ridden very recently by a child from a nearby riding school.

Ten minutes later, her suspicions were confirmed. There were the stables and in the yard, a pony having its saddle removed before being led back to its stall. In a paddock, out of view of the stable, a large thoroughbred mare was cropping weeds from under the gate.

Monti's eyes lit up. Here was her free taxi-ride home. She clicked her tongue softly. The horse stopped cropping and lifted its head with a snort. Monti huffed on its nose and it pleated its lips back, showing its large green teeth.

Monty felt in her bag and dropped the carrot in the grass. While it busied itself with the carrot, she climbed onto the gate and swung her leg over the mare's back. It put its head up sharply, but didn't object to her sitting there. It had read her mind anyway, and given the carrot it was more than happy to do her bidding.

With a cursory look over her shoulder, Monti leant forward, pushed the gate open and walked the horse through.

She steered it behind the stable block and then rode quietly through a gap in the trees, away from the beaten track. As soon as the hooves were out of earshot, she changed gear and galloped down the hill, across the valley and beyond.

By the time the stable owner discovered the mare was missing, it was out of the county.

As Monti approached the edge of the forest, the full moon appeared like a porch light, its billion-watt bulb welcoming her home.

The trees were ghostly with mist and, despite the considerable heat from the horse, she could have done with her old coat. She felt vulnerable without it. Apart from providing warmth and a certain dignity, it had contained most of her worldly goods, not to mention her hunting tools.

She was going to have to make a new coat and wondered how good Jimmy Scar was with a needle and cotton. There again, Jimmy Scar was probably too busy building her folly to agree to a sewing job.

Whatever, she was bound to have a fire going. The thought of a real fire filled Monti with glee. It had been unbearably hot in hospital. The heat from the radiators had baked the air until it was only fit for germs to breathe and this, she was convinced, was the reason for ninety per cent of the deaths on the ward.

The horse stopped.

'Trot on!'

But the mare refused. It had smelt the distinctive aroma of mule. Suddenly, there was a loud harrumph and a chunky, slab of a face appeared over a bush.

'Cecil B!' greeted Monti. 'My *dear* boy!'

She was pleased to see he had lost very little weight in her absence and, if possible, looked more handsome than ever. Cecil stared at her angrily and put his nose in the air.

'What?' said Monti. 'Now, look here! I didn't leave you on purpose.'

It wasn't that though. It was the arrival of the mare.

'Cecil, I do believe you're jealous,' she smiled, dismounting. 'This horse is a just a *convenience*, you are my very old *friend*.' She patted the mare on the rump. 'Off you go, dear!'

The mare refused to budge. For years it had ridden round and round in tedious circles with squealing children strapped to its back and pulling at its mouth. Today, it had galloped up hills and across fields. It had blown the hay dust from the bottom of its lungs and soared over high fences instead of soppy little black and white poles that wouldn't trip a Shetland.

'Geddalong, horse!'

Never! The mare dug her heels in and started flirting with Cecil. She liked him. He was different from those arrogant stallions. Cecil was amusing.

Monti left them to it and pushed her way into the clearing, whistling for Duke. The fact that he wasn't there didn't worry her. It was night time, he would be hunting.

It was only when she saw no fire had been made that she felt a chill of fear. It hadn't been made that day and it clearly hadn't been made for a long time.

'Jimmy Scar?'

Her first thought was that the girl might be ill or injured and was lying in the dwelling, unable to move, but then she noticed the shadow of her own petticoat hanging stiffly on the line. She had hung it out the morning before the storm. If the girl was at home, she'd have taken it in by now.

There were no bones in the clearing. No skins or pips,

no scrapings. No obvious signs of meals taken by human or dog.

Monti tore off the ivy that gripped the swollen door and pushed it open with a trembling hand. She was knocked out by the stale breath that hit her. Inside, there was pitch black silence.

Automatically, she reached for the tinderbox in her voluminous pannier to light a candle, but of course, she was wearing the gentleman's trousers and had no matches on her.

Leaving the door open, she let her eyes grow accustomed to the dark. The bed hadn't been slept in at all. The house hadn't been lived in and it seemed to be dying of neglect. Part of the roof had collapsed as if someone had jumped on it. Cobwebs hung like dirty net curtains and already, the horsetails had broken in.

Assuming that Jimmy and Duke had left her for dead, Monti did something she hadn't done since her mother was killed. She lay down and she cried.

In the cold light of the new morning, Monti reconsidered Jimmy's fate. With hindsight, the likelihood of her upping sticks like that was completely out of character.

She had nowhere to go, she was afraid of being recognised and captured and even if she *had* thought Monti was dead, she could have stayed and kept house in the forest for several months quite easily. There were plenty of provisions after all. She had the skills.

No, she decided. Jimmy's disappearance had been sudden. She had checked for recent tracks and there were none. On further investigation, she found a few preserved dog tracks heading away from the dwelling and while they weren't fresh, it suggested that Duke must have left some time after Jimmy and that for some reason, they had been split up.

A thorough search of the area convinced her that Jimmy was long gone and not dead in the undergrowth which could mean only one thing; she had been taken against her own will. The discovery of deep ruts in the turf left by the helicopter confirmed her worst suspicions.

It didn't take a great leap of the imagination for her to realise that Jimmy must have been the one to summon the emergency services and in saving Monti's life, had fallen into enemy hands. That's why the police had wanted to talk to her in hospital.

'Poor Jimmy Scar!' she fretted. 'She'll be like a squirrel in a cage and not a single living relative to save her.'

As she rode Cecil B back to the dwelling, she tried to think of a rescue plan. Given that the child could be anywhere in the country, she wasn't at all sure where to begin. Her recent foray into the outside world had convinced her that while she had managed to get back to the forest by the skin of her teeth, she hadn't got the skills to survive on the streets.

As she set to work fixing the collapsed roof, she wondered if it would be possible to adapt the rules of Coggins' Bible so that they applied in an urban situation. It worked up to a point. She could find or make a shelter and hunt for food using similar techniques. She could probably cope, but how could she track Jimmy Scar? She could hardly follow her footprints in the city.

'And which city, Cecil?' she sighed. 'There are so many and they are so very far apart. It is not as if I can go by mule!'

Cecil B wasn't listening. He nuzzled the refined nose of his new companion and huffed contentedly.

'You don't give a damn, do you?' said Monti. 'Ah, why should you, hmm? Why should *I* come to that?'

She started to pull the little forest of weeds out from the cracks between the stone floor and flung them into a basket. Monti, who had vowed never to get attached to anyone ever again was surprised to find how much Jimmy Scar meant to her.

Even so, she wished she'd never set eyes on her. Now she was compelled to feel disturbing emotions like concern and desperation all over again.

'Wretched child,' she snorted. 'Why couldn't you have been one of those unbearable little girls who don't like getting their hands dirty? Why come bothering me?'

She marched out with her basket of weeds and cast them in a heap a little distance away behind a bush. The bush was bare now.

'Blow you, Jimmy Scar!'

She kicked the fallen leaves up in frustration. They rose in a crackling cloud. It made her feel good, so she did it again and again until suddenly she noticed something gleaming on the ground. A coin . . . and there was another one. And another. It was the loose change Jimmy Scar had thrown over her shoulder!

Monti picked them up and rubbed the dust off and saw the matronly profile of the Queen on the tenpence piece.

'Ten *pence*? And is that . . . *Elizabeth*? Good heavens, she's ancient!'

Suddenly, it struck her that they were virtually the same age and that while the forest had hardly changed in the decades she'd been living there, the rest of the world, including the currency, had altered beyond recognition.

She was about to throw the money over her shoulder when she remembered what Jimmy Scar had said about trying to find her father. She would find the nearest telephone and ring round all the prisons!

Despite Monti's lifelong aversion to money, these coins were the very thing she needed to start her search.

Yes! She could take the riding school horse out into civilisation under cover of darkness and see if she could find a public telephone box – Cecil B would be no good, he would panic if a car went by. Then, she would phone... who? The prisons? The hospital? The police? And ask them what?

Here, the plan fell apart. She didn't know Jimmy Scar's real name. She could hardly ask the authorities if they knew the whereabouts of Jimmy Scar or her father, Mr Scar, because neither of them existed.

She thought maybe she could use the coins to buy the other thing she despised – a newspaper. But if Jimmy had been found and captured, it would be old news by now.

She shoved the coins into her pocket and went back indoors, frustrated and tired. Her burns were throbbing. She lay down and picked up her volume of *Sherlock Holmes*. The bookmark was still on page 323, from when she'd last read it to Jimmy. Sherlock Homes was talking to Doctor Watson in *The Adventure of The Berley Coronet*:

'...it is my belief, Watson, founded upon my experience, that the lowest and vilest alleys in London do not present a more dreadful record of sin than does the smiling and beautiful countryside...'

Monti frowned. She read the phrase over and over again. Here was a man who knew the city like the back of his hand! Here was the Charlie Coggins of the metropolis. The surest way to find Jimmy was to hire a detective like Holmes!

It would be a while before it was dark enough to venture out. Monti busied herself by adapting the tweed jacket she had stolen into something more useful. She lined it with rabbit fur, added part of a pleated wool skirt to the bottom and stitched several secret pockets inside.

Then, she tended to her burns. She had been treating them with various herbal ointments and they were a lot less angry-looking than they had been. There was nothing she could do about her limp. It came and went, depending on how much walking she did, so when it flared up, she swallowed powdered willow for the pain.

She had found her old tinderbox up on the hill, half-hidden under a coil of rotted grassrope. She also found the spade. The head had melted right down to the handle.

An owl hooted. She stuffed her pockets with new hooks, pins and string and slid her pistol into her belt. She lit a fresh tallow candle, took Cecil B's bridle from its hook and approached the riding school mare with a handful of nuts. Suspecting it might be taken back to the riding school, it turned its head away.

'No, we're not going there!' said Monti. 'Tell her, Cecil? I'll be back for you later.'

Cecil could detect a whiff of optimism above the smell of the hazelnuts and reassured the mare that Monti's intentions were good. After that, she allowed herself to be bridled and ridden away with no more fuss.

Monti found her way back to the village by the light of the stars. There was the post office and the greengrocer's stall, closed now, of course.

She had left the mare tied to a tree in the shadows of the deserted churchyard and walked the rest of the way. She remembered seeing a telephone box near a wrought-iron lamp and sure enough, there it was. There wasn't a soul about.

She entered the telephone box. It smelled of cigarettes, but not unpleasantly so. The fuggy warmth in there came as a relief. She began to turn the pages of a heavily-thumbed directory, running a shaking finger down the index marked D.

There were only a handful of detectives listed. Given the limited number of coins she had and not knowing how long she could speak for until her money ran out, she decided to go with the first one and hope for the best.

Having struggled to read the instructions above the telephone in the dim light, Monti cautiously lifted the receiver and dialled. A man's voice answered, dozy with sleep.

'Hello? This is Linden Spoke. What time is it?'

Chapter 14

Linden Spoke, otherwise known as Spook since his miserable schooldays, got into the minicab and instructed the driver to take him as near to the edge of the forest as it was possible to take a car.

'Bit early for a walk, mate, isn't it?' said the cabbie.

It was dark still.

'I'm meeting a client,' said Spook.

He saw the cabbie pull a face in the rear-view mirror.

'Say no more,' he said, and tapped his nose.

Spook fiddled in his briefcase nervously. He had been in a deep sleep when the phone rang. The old dear on the end of the phone had said it was a matter of urgency and instructed him to meet her by the fishing lake at five o'clock in the morning. He was to bring no one with him and for his troubles, he would be handsomely paid.

That was the lure of course – the money. Linden believed very strongly that if he had enough of it, he would instantly appear more attractive to others. He told himself that if only he could afford a flashy car, it would compensate for his lack of personality.

He had been fired from his job in the city because he hadn't fitted in. He was weak, wan and had the unfortunate posture of a hyena. That aside, what really set him apart was his failure to laugh at the laddish jokes of his colleagues. He was unable to join in with their male banter.

Linden was a mummy's boy. An only child and a late arrival at that, he had been cosseted for so long that by the time he should have left home, he could scarcely knot his own tie. He was twenty-five.

Terrified of his mother's disappointment, he never told her he'd been fired and continued to take the train to work every day so she wouldn't suspect. He had tried to get a job in a bookmaker's, because he was good at figures, but they had turned him down, as did the owner of an ice cream van, who told him he would scare away the younger customers.

While he was nursing a cold cup of tea in a scruffy café, he noticed an ad in the local paper suggesting he might be able to find employment as a detective. 'Be your own boss!' it had said. It appealed to Spook no end, because it meant he could work from home. He would no longer have to brave the brutal environment of the workplace. His asthma might even improve.

As he re-read the blurb, he also realised that given he had no life of his own to speak of, here was the perfect opportunity to live through other people's.

He immediately sent off for his free master detective package and received a rather flimsy book of tips and a free bugging device that broke as soon as he got it out of the bag. He read the book in five minutes flat and did as it advised, which was namely to advertise himself in a certain telephone directory for a large sum of money.

That had been a month ago, but no one had bothered to call. His services, it seemed, were not required and he had pretty much forgotten all about his new career until Monti called.

As luck would have it, his elderly mother was visiting

her niece at the time, so he was saved the task of having to explain where he was off to at that ridiculous hour of the morning. He almost phoned her out of sheer habit, just to let her know where he was, just in case. In case of what, he wasn't sure, but 'Just In Case' was his mother's motto.

'You should take a plastic mac, just in case,' she would say, on a baking July morning.

Linden found his pac-a-mac, had a quick suck of his inhaler, checked the gas was off three times and locked the front door behind him.

The minicab was slowing down. Linden's heart began to pound. The driver pulled over, left the engine running and turned to Spook.

'Can't get much nearer in than this, pal.'

'F... fine.'

It looked really dark out there. Linden had felt distinctly uneasy as soon as they'd left the town. He couldn't stand the countryside with its vast amounts of oxygen and great wastes of space. It made him feel exposed and small and he automatically wrapped his arms around his body to protect himself. He was reluctant to get out of the comforting confines of the car.

'That'll be twenty-five quid,' said the driver.

Linden sorted the paper notes out clumsily.

'Could you wait for me?' he asked.

The driver looked him up and down.

'Depends. How long a you gonna be.'

Linden wasn't sure.

'Please,' he said. 'I'll give you a tenner.'

The driver scoffed. 'Nothing doing, I've got another pick-up in half an hour.'

Linden got out of the car very slowly. He shivered and zipped his anorak up to his nose.

As the minicab disappeared into the mist, he felt as if he'd wandered onto the set of a horror movie and began to feel anxiously round for his inhaler.

He tiptoed gingerly among the skeletons of trees. He could feel the sweat soaking into his vest, despite the chill in the air. The sounds of the forest were making him extremely nervous, so in order to muffle them he'd withdrawn his ears so far inside his hood his face was barely visible.

Unfortunately, the padding in the hood distorted the sounds so much, they became even more terrifying. Every twig that cracked was the footstep of a mad axeman, every squeak of a bat the revengeful spirit of the dead.

By the time Monti found him, he was backed against a bush with his head between his knees, having a panic attack.

'Mr Spoke?'

He looked up at the wild spectre that confronted him and screamed. He wasn't an imaginative man, but his mother had brought him up on such grisly bedtime stories, he was convinced he'd been cornered by the ghost of some ghastly hag with a two-headed horse.

Monti dismounted. She took a brown paperbag out of her pocket, handed it to him and instructed him to breathe into it slowly. This he did without hesitation, as he was used to obeying older women automatically.

After a few gulps, he relaxed slightly, and the colour came back into his face.

'Better?' she asked.

He nodded feebly.

'I'm Monti.'

'Linden Spook... I mean Spoke.' He shook her hand limply. 'Master Detective.'

She put her hands on her hips and looked him up and down.

'Can you ride?'

His reached for the brown bag again. The question had started a whole new reason to panic.

'I've brought a horse and a mule. Which would you prefer?'

Linden sat with his knees somewhere around his chin in Monti's dwelling, the cheeks of his backside beaten and bruised by the long and painful journey on the back of Cecil B. He knew nothing about animals and as far as he was aware, mules were carnivorous.

Cecil, knowing the man couldn't ride, had been particularly wicked to him, dropping his head suddenly at one point, causing Spook to slide off his neck and land on his buttocks with the reins between his legs.

'Shall I brief you now?' asked Monti, handing him a piece of smoked meat.

He looked at it hungrily. 'Chicken?'

'Hedgehog, Mr Spoke.'

He gagged slightly, put the plate on the floor and took a pad of lined paper from his briefcase.

'First things first,' he said. 'I need to know your full title.'

Monti was amazed. She had taken the man for an idiot, yet he must be on the ball to have discovered she was a Duchess so quickly.

'How did you know I was titled?'

'What? No, no. I mean are you Mrs, Miss or Ms?'

'Ms?'

Monti had never heard of Ms.

'Are you married?'

She shook her head.

'I don't believe in it, do you?' she said.

Linden's face went scarlet. He mumbled something into his sleeve about girlfriends and mothers not approving of them.

'Ah!' she said. 'I quite understand, only in my case, it was Father.'

She told him the sorry tale of her lover and the baby and how happy they'd been in Paris, just the three of them, living in the blue room on the few centimes he earned as a labourer.

'But he would *insist* that we got married,' she said. 'He wanted so much for our son to inherit this land.'

Linden scribbled everything down on his pad.

'What land?' he said, without looking up.

'Why...this!' said Monti, making a broad gesture with her arms. 'My father owned all the land we rode through. He was the Duke!'

She told him how he'd shot her mother dead and how he'd died in prison from a lack of caviar and it was at that point Linden threw down his pen.

'Are you winding me up?' he said.

Right now, he had a nasty feeling he'd been dragged out of his warm, safe bed on the promise of riches by a mad woman.

'Am I lying, do you mean?' Monti was taken aback 'Why should I bother to lie? I told you I was titled, didn't I? Well, for your information, I am Diana, Duchess of Marley and somewhere out there and I don't know where, I have a son who will inherit the Dukedom upon my death.'

'Oh really?' said Linden, wearily.

'Yes, really! He's called James. There's no need to write it down. I don't need you to look for him, I need you to look for Jimmy Scar.'

'And he is . . . ?'

'He's a girl,' said Monti. 'I was struck by lightning and she's gone missing.'

By now, Linden was absolutely convinced of Monti's insanity and he thought in a mindless, unmeditated way that if there was any money to be had, he could go along with this madness and maybe con her out of it.

'I see,' he said. 'You realise I'll need some money up front.'

'Of course,' said Monti. 'Would you like it now? I hate the stuff myself, but if you can put it to good use and find Jimmy Scar, it's all yours.'

Linden sat with his mouth hanging open. Monti took an enormous toasting fork from the wall. 'Follow me!' she said.

Linden got up, as if in a trance, and lurched behind Monti into the wilderness, illuminated by the watery glow of the dawn.

'Where are we going? To the bank? Do you have a plastic card?'

She didn't answer. She was busy trying to remember where she'd buried the first lot of gold.

'It's round here *somewhere*,' she said after a while. 'Of course, I never thought I'd want to see it again so I never drew a map. Everything's so overgrown now...ah!'

She started to pace out a few metres from an old oak tree, then plunged her toasting fork into the soil.

'Here's some!' she said. 'I don't know if it's enough for you, Mr Spoke. If not, there are some rubies and what-have-you over yonder and rather a lot of silver and a few bonds down in the meadow.'

Linden peered into the shallow hole. It was stuffed with gold ingots. He stared in disbelief.

'This is yours?'

'Yes. Oh, yes, the place is riddled with it.'

She pulled a face.

'My son James is supposed to inherit the lot, but he knows nothing of his real station in life and that's the way it must stay. I don't care if that's illegal or not. I'm his mother and I'd hate him to become a money-grubber and a conman.'

Linden, who had been drooling at Monti's riches, put his tongue away and looked guiltily at his muddy shoes.

'Don't worry, Mr Spoke,' she added kindly. 'I am not talking about you in particular.'

Linden felt strangely tearful. This lady wasn't mad, not at all. She was a mother who loved her son so dearly, she'd gone to these bizarre lengths to protect him from her particular definition of evil.

In her case, it was money. In his mother's case, it was The Outside World. In both cases, he felt these enormous acts of kindness were causing untold damage and now he felt a creeping rage brighten his hollow, grey cheeks.

'What is it?' asked Monti. 'You seem...upset?'

Linden wasn't used to speaking his mind because he didn't have much of a mind to speak of, but now that he was out here in the open, he felt an uncharacteristic urge to have his say. It was rather like the urge he felt to jump onto the railway line when the train was coming.

'I can just about understand why you've denied your son vast amounts of money,' he blurted. 'What I can't understand is how you've denied him his *mother* for all these years.'

Monti was impressed. He was shaking with passion, looking her in the eye. She saw that his eyes were beautiful – deep brown, with a ring of gold around them, like an owl.

'You think I am heartless, Mr Spoke?'

Linden nodded and sat down hard. Monti sat next to him.

'Mr Spoke, if you had been denied your mother, do you think you might have been a happier person?'

There was another long silence. Linden tried not to think about the many times he'd wished his mother dead for turning him into what he'd become: lonely except in her company; a failure in everybody's eyes, except hers. Those were the chains that bound him to her. Now she was frail, there was no breaking away.

'My mother loves me,' he said flatly. 'I really ought to be getting back.'

He scrabbled to his feet, determined to go.

'Mothers can love too much,' called Monti. 'I thought we had a business arrangement.'

He was walking away. 'I'm not up to it.'

'Says who? You or your mother, Mr Spoke?'

'I'm cold.'

'So we'll make a fire. Do you know how to make a fire?'

He stopped walking. His mother had never let him join the Boy Scouts. She didn't want him to go to camp just in case he fell in the river and drowned. Just in case he was charged by a bull. Just in case! Just in case!

'I'll show you how,' said Monti.

He followed her home like a lamb. Linden spread out his plastic mac and sat on it in the clearing, ready to be waited on.

'You need to fetch the wood,' said Monti. 'It's over there, under cover.'

'What . . . me? I'm not dressed for it. This is my best anorak! What about splinters?'

He made a hundred excuses.

'I thought you were cold,' she said. 'You don't want to build a fire? That's fine by me. You do what you want to do.'

He pulled a sulky face. He desperately wanted to build a fire, but there were going to be spiders in that woodpile, he just knew it. If one ran over his hand, he'd probably throw up.

'Jimmy Scar was good at making fires,' called Monti. 'She was a natural. I've never seen a girl handle wood like she did.'

Linden was jealous of girls. It was too hard, being a man. It seemed that everybody expected men to behave in a certain way, even if they didn't say it out loud, yet girls had choices. They could like spiders or be scared of them, be good at woodwork or not; both things were acceptable in a girl. Encouraged even. But in a boy? He thought not.

He moved one of the logs with the end of his shoe to

make sure there were no creepy crawlies under it and picked it up. He was unused to carrying anything much heavier than his wallet and his legs sagged under the weight.

'Back straight, bend your knees,' said Monti. 'Lift with your belly muscles.'

Linden didn't have any. Monti watched him and tried to imagine how he might look, given enough fresh air and exercise. She decided he could be almost good-looking.

'Jimmy Scar was going to build her own dwelling in the woods,' she said. 'She inherited her building skills from her father. It was going to be a surprise for him when he got out of prison.'

Linden staggered across the clearing with the log, panting.

'Why was he in prison? Bit of a rogue, was he?'

Monti pursed her lips. 'Not at all. He was trying to rescue his daughter's dog.'

She went into great detail about Mr Kasheffi and how Jimmy Scar had run away with Duke and ended up living in the forest. As Linden listened and asked questions, he forgot to feel self-conscious about handling the logs and found he was getting the hang of it.

'Her mother was killed when she was a baby,' concluded Monti.

'Yeah? She sounds like the kid in the Diamond case,' said Linden carelessly, admiring his muddy trouser knees.

'The what?'

'You know. It was in all the papers. You must have read about it.'

Monti shook her head excitedly. 'I don't get the

papers. I didn't even look at them in hospital when I was struck by lightning!'

Linden dropped the log on his foot. He screwed his eyes up and looked at her sideways.

'Struck by . . . ? ' he said. 'You . . . ? I do *not* believe this! You're the old tramp rescued by the helicopter, aren't you?'

'Tramp?' snorted Monti.

He was trying to remember something. He paced about, then clicked his fingers triumphantly.

'Got it! "***Little Lady and the Tramp!***" That was the headline. The missing girl came with you. She was recognised by the pilot.'

'She was? Was she about ten years old with dark, curly hair?'

'Scar down one side of her face,' added Linden, nodding vigorously.

Monti clapped her hand to her mouth. 'That's Jimmy Scar . . . ' she breathed. 'Mr Spoke, that's my Jimmy Scar!'

He shook his head. 'No. That's Gemma Diamond.'

Chapter 15

'Mr Spoke, are you absolutely sure about the missing girl's surname?' asked Monti.

He nodded. 'It was definitely Diamond,' he said. 'A quick phone call to the newspaper and we can find out his whereabouts and possibly hers. We could have this all put to bed by...er...bedtime, Mrs...Duchess?' He wasn't at all sure how to address this unusual client of his anymore.

She had unpinned her brooch and was gazing at the photo of the man holding her child.

'He always called me Monti,' she said. 'It was his joke, you see.'

Linden was still trying to light the fire and wasn't listening properly.

'I don't get it,' he mumbled. 'I haven't got much of a sense of humour.'

Monti clapped her hands together sharply, extinguishing the flame as it crept up his last matchstick.

'Oh, do keep up, Mr Spoke. My name's *Di*ana – *Di*- amanté. Only he pronounced it *monti*,' she explained. 'A diamanté is a fake diamond. If I'd married Will, I would have been a *real* Diamond. Diamond was his surname.'

Linden still wasn't concentrating.

'Yeah? Oh, now I've run out of matches.'

Monti threw him the tinderbox.

'This Gemma Diamond,' she said. 'What was her

father called? Can you remember?'

'Er…' Linden scraped away at the tinderbox. 'Dopey, was it? Dippy? No, Dodgy Diamond!'

'*Dodgy*?'

'Yeah. That's what the papers nicknamed him.' He rocked back on his heels.

'That's it! "Dodgy Diamond's Little Gem Does Runner." Only his real name was Jim, I think.'

Monti thrust the oval, faded photo of her son in his face. 'His real name was *James*!'

Linden's hand slipped so violently mid-strike, he created his first spark with the tinderbox. He took the brooch and studied the photo. He looked down at the child. He looked up at Monti. The family likeness was unmistakable.

'Gemma Diamond's father is your *son*?'

'But can we prove it, Mr Spoke?'

It only took a couple of phonecalls on Linden's mobile to find out where Jim Diamond had been incarcerated.

The journalist who'd written the newspaper articles gave him the name of the prison in exchange for the possibility of an interview. Linden had agreed but at Monti's suggestion, he gave a false name and address.

'My name? It's…it's Mr Leonard Spike. Where do I live? Um…'

He put his hand over the receiver as Monti mouthed a helpful suggestion.

'Number One, Forest Way, Linden-on-Sea.'

He repeated the bogus address into the phone and rang off with a sigh. Monti patted him on the back.

'Well done. The last thing we want is the press

crawling all over us. I'll make you some breakfast while you phone the prison.'

'Have you got any All-Bran, only I'm a bit bunged up,' he admitted, rubbing his stomach. 'I think it's all the excitement.'

'Rhubarb and sorrel!' announced Monti. 'That should shift it, Mr Spoke.'

Linden smiled hopefully and jabbed at his mobile again.

The prison was able to confirm that Prisoner 87479 was indeed detained at Her Majesty's pleasure, awaiting trial and if a visit was required, then an order could be posted.

'Thanks a lot. Yep . . . yeah . . . and if you could send it to Number One, Forest Way . . . '

Monti shook her head violently. 'Give them your real address or it'll never arrive!'

Ten minutes easy work and they had already found Jim. Finding Gemma was proving more difficult.

After demolishing his toasted rhubarb and sorrel cakes, Linden phoned Social Services, but they refused to part with any information on the grounds that he wasn't a relative.

'But I am!' Monti insisted.

'Yeah, but they want *proof*. Have you got James's birth certificate?'

Her face fell. 'I think it's in Paris.'

'Oh, dear.'

Linden had only ever been abroad once, to Belgium, and had vowed never to do it again. Apart from his agoraphobia, the lurching of the sea had turned his stomach inside out and he'd embarrassed himself over the side of the ferry and all down his trousers.

But now he'd discovered he could make a fire, he was brimming with new confidence and found himself thinking that if he went via Eurotunnel, Paris might be rather jolly.

'*Parlez-vous français*, Mr Spoke?'

'Er... Non. J'ai terrible at it.'

What did it matter if he could barely speak the lingo? Once he'd found the building where they registered births, deaths and marriages, all he had to do was give the clerk the name he was after, pay for a copy and thank him for it. *Merci, monsieur*. It hardly required a degree in French.

'I'll go!' he said.

'It'll take days by ship!' wailed Monti.

'A day,' corrected Linden. 'If I go through the tunnel.'

And he explained in boring detail about the railway under the Channel that linked Britain to France. Monti found it all very hard to believe, but as she was in no position to doubt him, she insisted he take some of the gold bars and be on his way.

'I'll have to exchange these at your bank first,' he said.

'But I don't have a bank.'

He spent the next hour on the phone trying to sort something out.

'They need deeds, details, death certificate...' he told her, holding his hand over the mouthpiece.

'All in a biscuit tin,' she said.

'Pass it to me, then.'

'I can't, Mr Spoke. It's buried in the meadow.'

Linden Spoke made a gesture of exasperation with both hands. He'd never made that gesture before, but now he felt he was in charge, it came as naturally as it did to those lads in the city.

Monti took her toasting fork and left him to it. By the time she came back with the rusty tin full of documents, he was raring to go. A minicab would be waiting for him at the edge of the forest.

'I've booked my seat on the train,' he said. 'Now I need to go home, fetch my passport, go to the bank . . . have you written a covering letter, Monti?'

She handed him a piece of paper, torn from her prized volume of *Sherlock Holmes*.

There was an illustration of the detective on the back, crouching down with a magnifying glass.

'I thought it might inspire you,' she said. 'Have you spoken to your mother?'

He hadn't, but he had phoned the house where she was staying to speak to his cousin, Alicia. She was a solicitor and they were going to need one. His mother had wanted to speak to him but he'd braced himself, said he was in a hurry and asked Alicia to send her his love. Just in case. He gave Monti Alicia's phone number.

'Ring up and ask for Miss Alicia Spoke,' he said. 'I've put her in the picture as best as poss. but she needs to talk to you. She's agreed to represent Jim. She'll be able to arrange a visit for you if you like.'

Monti brushed something from her eye. She wondered whether or not James would want to see her. She wasn't sure he knew she was alive. He would blame her for everything that had gone wrong, because that's what children did. Perhaps they did it with good reason.

'I'll give you a lift to the minicab,' she said. 'If your buttocks are up to it.'

'My buttocks are fine,' announced Spoke.

As he walked away, shoulders back and head held high, Monti had to admit they were.

Monti was just about to shoot her dinner when the mobile phone rang. The rabbit, extremely grateful for modern technology, kicked up its legs and disappeared down the nearest hole.

'Beggar!'

Monti looked at the piece of black, bleeping plastic helplessly. Which button was it she was supposed to press? Mr Spoke had shown her, but it hadn't sunk in. She prodded about haphazardly and the phone went dead.

'Ah, it's broken,' she said. 'I never could see how it could work without a wire.'

She shoved it back in her pocket and was just about to make her way home when it rang again. This time, she pressed the right button and held it to her ear.

'Hello?'

A voice seemed to be calling from somewhere down near her chin. The phone was upside down.

'Mr Spoke, is that you?'

'Yes!'

'What... calling all the way from Paris?'

She couldn't believe it and shook the phone, as if that might somehow make it more real.

'Monti? Can you hear me? I've got James's birth certificate... Father, William Diamond... Mother, Lady Diana Marley. Baby's date of birth, 5th of October 1957.'

The fifth of October 1957! It had been the most

golden day. James had been born with little fuss in the blue room, with an old French midwife who couldn't speak a word of English but understood everything. Will had held him, still sticky and wet from the world he'd just come from and brushed his lips on the soft patch on the top of the baby's head.

'Monti . . . are you there?'

'Just taking a trip down memory lane, Mr Spoke.'

Now it was his turn to go quiet. Until now, he hadn't had any memories worth making a trip for, but he wouldn't forget this one in a long time.

'Mr Spoke, are you there? How is Paris?'

'It's fantastic!' he said. 'I had a cup of coffee on the pavement and I didn't get palpitations. Oh and your rhubarb and sorrel worked. My mum would have a fit if she saw the state of the toilets here. I've visited seven already.'

Monti laughed out loud. 'Better out than in, Mr Spoke! What happens next?'

'I think I'll go mad and order one of those chocolate croissants, Monti.'

'No, no, what happens with the birth certificate?'

He said he'd faxed a copy to Alicia, the solicitor.

'You've done what with it?'

'Faxed it . . . Oh, never mind. She's got a copy. She'll take it to Social Services and hopefully they'll tell her where Gemma is . . . Pardon, did you say something? This line's terrible, Monti. You're breaking up.'

'Yes, I think I probably am,' she spluttered, dabbing her eyes. 'Mr Spoke . . . Linden?' But he'd gone. Monti wasn't sure what she thought of the mobile phone. When someone was speaking, it seemed like a living thing and she liked it, but the minute the voice had gone, it was dead. Cold. She stuffed it back in her pocket.

When it rang again, it startled her. She almost dropped it in her haste to put it to her ear.

'Yes... yes... Hello? You sound funny, Mr Spoke. Have you got your mouth full of croissant?'

There was a pause.

'This is Miss Spoke, Mr Linden Spoke's cousin? I've found out where Gemma is.'

Alicia put the receiver down and smiled. She'd had the craziest conversation with the old Duchess. The story was like something out of a romantic novel. She had been in two minds about getting involved, but now she wanted to know how the story was going to end.

She'd had a long chat with Linden beforehand. At first, she couldn't believe it was him on the phone. He sounded nothing like the wimpy younger cousin she remembered.

She'd teased him about his new career. Him a detective? What kind of job was *that*? Had he been reading too many comics? But for the first time ever, he'd teased her back. He'd said, 'Get a life, Alicia.'

She'd protested. She said she had a brilliant career, a wonderful flat, a big car and designer clothes. What had *he* ever achieved? And he'd said, 'I have discovered fire.'

She hadn't realised he'd simply learnt a basic Boy-Scout skill. She thought he was implying something far deeper. She thought he'd discovered a new kind of passion, something that had set his heart alight and she was deeply jealous.

'I have ridden on the back of a mule and seen a new dawn,' he'd said.

She searched for the hidden meaning in that too. She assumed it was some reference to his mother. He was trying to tell her that he had finally thrown off the burden of being somebody's child and gone his own way. Or found God. Or possibly both.

She smoothed down her Maxmara suit, got into her Mercedes sports car and stopped and started through the stinking traffic all the way to the prison.

'Why do I do this?' she thought, strumming her fingers on the steering wheel. She shouted at the driver in front.

'Oh, come *on*!'

She hated wearing high-heeled shoes. They pinched, but they looked the part and she had to look the part.

'The light is on *green*, for God's sake.'

She only did all this to please her father. The job. The car. The suit. The flat. She wanted him to be proud of her, but he only ever had eyes for her older sister. Whatever she did was perfect.

'Look, just *go*, will you? Go! Go! GO! I haven't got all day!'

Now she'd got it all, she didn't want any of it. She wasn't happy. Her feet hurt. She wanted to jack it all in, but now she couldn't afford to. She parped her horn loudly.

'Move it!'

The woman in front had a baby. It was crying and she was turning round to comfort it.

'That's it! Cause an accident, you stupid...!'

Alicia wondered what it would be like to have a baby. Then she wondered what it must be like to have a baby that was involved in an accident. She thought of Jim Diamond and his daughter and how special it would be when they saw each other again. She even felt jealous of them, because she had never experienced that aching kind of love. It made her feel as empty and useless as a cracked vase.

In her job, she could change a person's life forever, but no one offered to change hers. She wished what she did for people would guarantee an emotional prize, but whether she lost or won their case, her reward was always the same. Money. And that was beginning to feel more and more like failure.

'A cuddle would be nice,' she thought. 'Or a meal for two.' But she was too professional to find time for either. That was, until she met Jim.

The minute she saw him, she felt as if she knew him. She'd seen his photo in the paper of course, but it was nothing to do with recognising his face – it was something more than that. Her voice wavered slightly as she spoke to him.

'Hello, Mr Diamond. I'm Alicia Spoke. I've been appointed to speak in your defence at the trial.'

She held out her hand. He stood up and shook it politely and even though he'd been ill, Alicia could feel the strength in it.

'Mr Diamond, I have something to tell you of great importance. Erm, you might like to sit down.'

The colour drained from his face. 'Gemma? Has something happened to Gemma?'

Quite against protocol, she touched his arm to reassure him. Shocked by her sudden lack of professionalism, she cleared her throat loudly.

'No, no. Gemma is safe and well...'

She watched all the muscles relax in his face. What lovely green eyes. He sighed almost imperceptibly, but she felt it like a blast.

'What is it, then?'

Alicia, aware that she's been staring at him, quickly lowered her eyes. She was looking for the right words. Which order should they go in. Should the word 'alive' or 'mother' or 'Duchess' come first.

'Your mother...' she began.

He put his head on one side, like a dog listening for a shepherd's whistle.

'My mother?'

'Yes, you see, my cousin is a detective and your mother hired him to...er...'

Jim frowned. 'My mother?' he said. 'Sorry, I think you might have got the wrong man because my mother's dead. She died when I was born.'

Linden hadn't bothered to mention the fact that Jim thought his mother was dead. Alicia fiddled with her papers, rearranged them and dropped them on the floor.

'No, um...actually she didn't. You see...'

'Yes, yes, she did, because my father, Will – well, he brought me up on his own.'

He was explaining it to her quite calmly, as if she had read the wrong notes. Alicia tried to compose herself.

'Mr Diamond...'

'Jim. Call me Jim.'

He was only trying to put her at ease but she felt her face starting to flush.

'Jim. Okay. Do you remember reading the newspaper when Gemma was found?'

'Yes. I kept it.'

'And you remember that she was found with an elderly lady who had been struck by lightning?'

'The tramp?'

'Yes. Well, that woman is your mother.'

'My mother is a tramp?'

Alicia tucked a loose strand of gold hair behind her ear and shook her head quickly.

'Oh, *no*. No, your mother's a Duchess.'

Jim started to laugh.

'No. You're having me on.'

'Really. I wouldn't joke about such serious matters, honestly. It's not ethical.'

'I'm the son of a Duchess! She's alive?'

'Yes.'

He wouldn't believe it. It was madness.

'I'm the son of a Duchess?'

'Yes. Jim, I realise this must all have come as a great shock. Your mother wants to see you . . . um . . . but she's afraid that after all these years . . .'

Jim bit his lip. Suddenly, he was a little boy who needed his mother. She wanted to fold him in her arms.

'I'm afraid too, Alicia,' he said.

Chapter 16

The manageress of Park View tapped on Gemma's bedroom door. There was no reply. Gemma didn't want to speak to anyone.

Although she had the run of the home, she wasn't interested in the collection of games in battered boxes or the table tennis table or the small garden. She had decided to imprison herself in her room.

She'd visited her father. She'd done as she was told and not attempted to escape because the threat of losing her visiting order had been real. She'd tried to be civil to the staff and even sat with the other children and watched television quietly in the communal room.

Although it was supposed to be a caring, family environment, the other kids referred to each other as inmates. They had little in common with each other, except that they were all unhappy and wanted to be with their parents, even the ones who had been abused. Any parent was better than none.

The previous Sunday, she was told that Clarice, one of the carers, was free to take her to the prison the next afternoon. Gemma was beside herself with excitement. She'd had a bath and washed her hair. She'd laid her clothes out on her bed and tried to decide which her father would like best. Should it be something girlish to reassure him nothing had really changed? Or something that showed how independent she'd become?

The only clothes that felt right were her cut-off shorts and T-shirt. In those, she was the real Gemma. Gemma of the Forest, Survivor, Life-saver! She wanted him to see her like that.

Clarice had other ideas. She threw her hands up in the air.

'Put something smart on, child!' she said. 'Your father will think we can't look after you properly!'

'I can look after myself,' she said.

'Sure you can,' said Clarice. 'Put this dress on, honey. You want to look your best, don't you?'

Gemma pulled the dress on miserably. It was old-fashioned. It was the kind of dress little girls wore to parties and she felt ridiculous.

'I can't wear this!'

'It just needs proper shoes. Take your trainers off. All you girls in your trainers! Men like to see a nice pair of shoes.'

She found Gemma some tights and a pair of black, patent shoes with a small heel. Gemma could feel the shape of the feet that had worn them before her. She couldn't walk in them properly.

'They don't fit.'

'They only seem that way after the trainers. They're your size.'

Clarice talked non-stop all the way to the prison. She rattled on about people Gemma had never heard of, friends of Clarice's who had done a certain thing or had a strange disease or had a bad experience at the dentist.

Gemma sat in the back of the car and tried to think what she was going to say to her father, but it was impossible.

'You're quiet, honey,' Clarice said. 'Are you nervous? I had an aunt who suffered with her nerves and she always used to say, "Clarice, if it wasn't for *boiled* sweets, I'd be in an asylum by now, with my nerves."'

'Really?' said Gemma, dully.

'Yes, she would suck the boiled sweets to calm herself down. Used to get through a pound bag a day!'

As Clarice expanded on the state of her aunt's teeth, Gemma found herself drifting off. The constant flow of chatter washed over her in sleep-inducing waves and she felt her eyes closing. She was jerked awake by Clarice's violent application of the handbrake.

'We're here!'

She took a comb out of her handbag and raked it through Gemma's fringe without asking.

'That's more like it. Now let's see a smile.'

Gemma, frowsy with sleep, fixed an empty grin on her face and followed Clarice through the prison gates.

There was an electric fence around the top of the high wall. She thought of the conversations she'd had with Monti about the cruelty of trapping animals and decided that this place, with its wire and spikes was more evil than anything Charlie Coggins could devise.

She thought she would be allowed to see her father on her own, but this wasn't to be. Clarice had to be with her. Those were the rules.

After they'd been searched, they were shown to a place like a school canteen with lots of tables and chairs. There was somewhere to get a drink and a snack. Clarice paid for a cup of tea and bought Gemma some crisps and a Coke.

'We'll have a little party,' she said.

Some party. There were uniformed guards standing at the back. Gradually, men wearing green prison tabards over their clothes drifted in and scanned the room expectantly for visitors. Gemma wondered what each of them had done.

Only one or two looked like criminals. The rest looked like people's fathers, grandads and brothers. Normal, everyday men for whom life had gone horribly wrong somewhere along the line.

Gemma sat down at an empty table and sipped her Coke nervously. They could only stay for an hour. She hoped he wouldn't be late. She was busy trying to open her crisps when he arrived. She hadn't seen him at first.

'Hi, Gem.'

She looked up with her mouth full of crisps.

'Give me those!' laughed Clarice. She took the crisps and started scrubbing at Gemma's face with a hanky, like she was a little kid with ice cream round her face.

'Sorry about that, Mr Diamond. You know what girls are!'

Gemma wanted to hit her. She'd made her look like a fool. She was ruining the moment. Gemma had counted off every hour of every day waiting to see her father and now this woman was destroying everything.

'Tell your daddy what you've been up to,' she coaxed.

Gemma had planned everything she was going to say. She was dying to tell him about the house she was building and how she'd lived in the wild and could track a deer and strip down a gun and...'

'Tell him about the table tennis, Gemma!' said Clarice. 'She had a little bit of trouble settling,' she told Jim, 'but she's doing fine now.'

Jim wanted to push the woman aside, jump over the table and pull his daughter into his arms. Right now, she couldn't even look at him.

'I got your letter, Gem. That was really nice.'

She'd written to him, but it was an empty kind of letter. She'd only said about the children's home and what she'd been doing there, because that's what they'd told her to put. She wasn't allowed to stick the envelope down because the prison officers had to be able to read it. You couldn't put anything private.

'How's Duke?'

'I don't know.'

She thought he'd be cross because she'd lost him. He'd think she couldn't look after anything. And after all he'd been through for that dog. It was all her fault he was in this terrible place. He must hate her.

'I'm so sorry, Dad.'

She started to cry. She tried to do it quietly so no one would notice, but she became hysterical. People were staring and Clarice panicked. She pulled Gemma into her chest and began to drag her away.

'I thought it was a bit too soon to come. We'll come back another time. Sorry about this, Mr Diamond.'

Jim reached out and grabbed Gemma's hand, which was dangling limply under Clarice's arm.

'Gem, please don't... it'll be okay.'

He felt her fingers curl round his thumb, the same reflex action she'd made when she was a newborn baby.

'I think we'd better cut this short,' said Clarice. 'Do it another time when Gemma's feeling stronger. Let's go now, Gemma, you're upsetting your dad.'

She pulled her away.

In the car on the way home, Clarice was hostile. Gemma had embarrassed her. What was all that noisy crying for? If Clarice had known there were going to be tears, she would never have brought her. It reflected badly on her professional judgement and that of the Children's Home. Now she would have to write a report.

'Prison visits!' Clarice snorted. 'A child shouldn't be subjected to the prison environment, no way. Who knows what all those men had been up to?'

'My father is innocent!' Gemma sobbed.

'Yes, well that's what they all say, honey. We'll see what they have to say at the trial.'

Gemma blew her nose and sat up straight.

'When he tells them about Duke and Mr Kasheffi and everything they'll have to let him go.'

Clarice shook her head.

'Uh...uh. You know, they might not. You have to prepare yourself for that, Gemma.'

Gemma had never believed for one minute that her father wouldn't be set free. It was impossible, surely, for someone to be given a prison sentence if they'd done nothing wrong?

'Prisons are full of people who've done nothing wrong,' said Clarice. 'It's all down to what the jury believe at the trial.'

Gemma went pale.

'Don't you worry, we'll look after you if the worst happens,' said Clarice, softening a little. Gemma shrank down in the car seat.

'Look at it this way...' continued Clarice. 'Say your old man got three years? He could be out after a year for good behaviour. Especially if it's his first offence.'

'But he hasn't done anything wrong, you silly old cow!' screeched Gemma.

Clarice glared at her. 'Pardon me?'

Gemma turned her head away.

'*Nothing*,' she whimpered.

'I should think so, young lady!'

Gemma didn't speak to anyone again all that week. She stayed in her room except for mealtimes, just like her father.

The manageress knocked on her door again, much louder this time. 'I wish you'd open the door, Gemma,' she said. 'You have a very important visitor. I can't send her away.'

Gemma, angry and sullen as she tried to sound, was intrigued. She racked her brains to think who on earth it could be. Her old school teacher, perhaps? Or Mrs Ellis? She broke her vow of silence.

'Who is it?'

'It's your grandmother.'

Gemma frowned. She got up and opened the door.

'Who did you say?'

The manageress was smiling at her kindly.

'Your grandmother.' She put her hand on Gemma's shoulder. Gemma shrugged it away, afraid it was just a cruel joke, a way of making her come downstairs and join in with the other children.

'I haven't got a grandmother.'

The woman held out her hand. 'Yes, you have, dear. Come with me. She's waiting for you in my office.'

She led Gemma down the stairs. One of the other children, a Turkish boy, called out as she passed, 'Are you going home then?' She paused and shrugged, confused.

'If not, I give you a game of ping pong.'

It was the first time he'd spoken to her all the time she'd been there. The manageress held the door of her office open.

'Go in, dear.'

There was someone in a tweed cap sitting in a swivel chair with her back to the door. At first, Gemma thought it was a man.

'Jimmy Scar?'

The person swung round to face her. Gemma let out a short, high-pitched cry.

'Monti . . . ? Oh, *Monti*!'

The manageress closed the door quietly and packed Gemma's things.

Gemma had her first decent night's sleep in ages back at the dwelling. There had been so much to talk about, they hadn't gone to bed until one. Finally, Monti pulled the tapestry blanket over her and kissed her forehead.

'Welcome home, Jimmy Scar.'

'Grandma, we *will* be able to get Dad out of prison, won't we?'

'We have the best solicitor money can buy,' she said. 'And stop calling me Grandma. It makes me feel old!'

Gemma grinned. 'Money isn't so terrible after all, is it, *Monti*?'

'Ah!' said Monti. 'I knew you'd say that and I've decided it rather depends who's spending it. Fancy a few pages of Holmes?'

She picked up the tattered volume. 'If it hadn't been for the master detective, I'd never have found you,' she said. 'Just you wait until you meet Mr Spoke.'

'Is he nice?'

Monti chuckled. Dear Mr Spoke. He was a changed man. He liked to stay with Monti, because he needed an excuse to make fires. He really got a kick out of chopping wood. He laid into it with such gusto that Monti had more logs than she knew what to do with.

'I owe him a great deal,' she said.

'Of money?'

'Of respect. Even Cecil respects him now.'

Cecil had behaved in a ludicrous fashion when Gemma first returned. Monti had warned her that he had a new girlfriend and might have forgotten all about her, but this wasn't the case.

The moment he saw her, he flared his nostrils and sucked the air in noisily through the great, damp holes. Then, to the embarrassment of the riding school mare, he threw himself onto his back and kicked his legs in the air like a foal, showing his teeth and giggling until his mouth was a bag of froth. Gemma had roared with laughter and scratched his belly with a stick.

'You silly old mule! . . . You *silly* old mule!'

'Really, Cecil B,' Monti remarked, drying her eyes. 'Anyone would think both your parents were donkeys!'

That night, as Gemma gazed up at the ceiling lights formed by the soft beams of stars shining through the leaf tiles, she announced she was as happy as anyone could possibly be . . . except for one thing.

'Duke,' said Monti.

'Do you think he's still alive?' Gemma sighed.

Monti put the book down and looked out of the window.

'Why shouldn't he be?' she said. 'He's a survivor. He

can hunt, he can hide, he's intelligent and strong.'

'Like me.'

'Quite. You came back, didn't you?'

Gemma nodded. Maybe he would come back. Maybe he was looking for her right now.

'Now go to sleep, Jimmy Scar. We have an early start in the morning if you're serious about wanting to give that nice man his twenty pounds back. What was his name again?'

'Ted,' said Gemma.

They took the train to Ted's.

'Why don't we get a taxi?' Gemma said. 'I'm not sure it's a very good idea to carry all that money about, Monti.'

Linden Spoke had given Monti an old, wicker shopping trolley on wheels that used to belong to his mother. He was concerned about Monti's limp and thought it might be useful for carting heavy objects about in. It had a plastic cover, a bit like a shower cap that you could pull over it to keep the rain off.

Monti was furious at the suggestion that she might not be as fit as she had been. Nevertheless, she was delighted with the basket and filled it with the strings of pearls, jewels, sovereigns and silver she had dug out of the meadow.

On top of that were great wads of notes, the thickness of bricks, that Linden had exchanged for the gold bars at the bank.

'I don't want to go in a taxi,' said Monti. 'I want to go by train. I've never been on one before.'

'What, *never*?'

'Ever been in a Rolls-Royce, Jimmy Scar?'

Gemma shook her head.

'Would you like to?'

'Yes, but I've never had a chance.'

'Well,' said Monti. 'I've never had the chance to go on a train.'

She loved every minute of it. 'I could do this every day!' she said.

Gemma smiled. Monti had her nose pressed to the window like a little girl.

'You wouldn't if you had to.'

The train plunged into a tunnel with a rush, and for a moment, the light flickered and went out. Monti panicked and clutched Gemma's hand. 'Aghhh! It's the end of the world!'

'It's a *tunnel*, Monti. The light will come back on in a minute.'

It was funny how everything had turned round. Monti had entered Gemma's world now and it was as confusing and alien to her as the forest had first seemed to the little city girl.

It was a much shorter walk from the station to Ted's than Gemma remembered. She hoped he'd be in. She wanted so much for him to know she wasn't a thief and to give him his money back.

'He hasn't got much,' said Gemma.

'Maybe he doesn't want much,' replied Monti. 'What a tiny little house!'

'It's a normal-sized house,' insisted Gemma.

They pressed the doorbell. He didn't answer it. It crossed Gemma's mind that he might be dead. He was very old. It was a possibility.

'He's not dead,' said Monti. 'He's sweeping up

leaves out the back.'

Gemma raised her eyebrows. 'How do you know?'

'Stands to reason,' said Monti. 'You said he was a keen gardener. There are leaves everywhere. This is the first time the wind has dropped in days. He'll be sweeping up.'

The door opened and Ted scowled at Monti.

'Didn't hear you,' he said. 'I was out the back, sweeping. If you're selling anything, I don't want it. If you've come to talk about God, forget it. I've already spoken to him, thank you very much.' He was about to close the door.

'Ted?' said Gemma. 'It's me, Jimmy Scar!'

He peered at Gemma and rubbed his eyes. His face broke into a broad smile.

'Aye aye?' he said. 'Didn't recognise you! Hee hee! You've grown your hair! Come in, come in!'

'This is my grandma.'

'Come in, gel.'

Ted shook her so warmly by the hand, she thought her arm was going to come off. Monti had never seen the inside of an ordinary person's house before. The closest she came to it was in Paris, and that was one room, but it had been a beautiful room, with fine furniture and oil paintings on the wall.

Ted put the kettle on and got out his best china cups. They were chipped and stained, but they were his best.

'I wish I'd known you were coming,' he said. 'I'd have got some biscuits. Come into the lounge.'

Monti sat awkwardly on the old sofa. The carpet was threadbare in places and there were dreadful prints of badly-drawn flowers in plastic frames.

‘Good paintings, aren’t they?’ he said.

‘I love flowers,’ said Monti, diplomatically.

‘I’ll show you my dahlias in a minute,’ said Ted. ‘We’ve been lucky. No frost so far.’

He prodded Gemma’s shoulder to get her attention.

‘Here, I never told those coppers you robbed my twenty quid,’ he said. ‘I told them I’d asked you to go shopping for me, that’s all. I couldn’t believe how they twisted it in the paper.’

‘You can’t trust a word they say,’ said Monti.

‘I’ve been worried stiff!’ he said. ‘You thinking I was a liar and dropping you in it.’

Gemma took a twenty-pound note out of her pocket and tried to give it to him. She thought he would be pleased, but he wasn’t.

‘Put it away, I don’t want it,’ he said.

‘Please!’ insisted Gemma.

He walked away. Gemma appealed to Monti for help, but Monti was looking out of the window at the garden. It was a masterpiece, the colours blended and swirled in a rich palette of russet, copper and bronze.

And there were the dahlias, their great lion’s heads rising proudly above the soil, stems straight, leaves saluting the wintry sun. Maybe they were all the gold he needed.

Gemma followed Ted and tried to put the money in his hand. ‘Please, Ted!’

He folded his arms.

‘How much did the shopping come to?’

Gemma did a quick sum. Paper, dog food, milk . . . cereal. ‘Er . . . about four pounds, I think.’

‘All right, say I give you a pound for going. Come

here by train today, did you? Right, so knock the fare off and you owe me...'

He scratched his head and pretended to add it up.

'Oh, I dunno. Give us a tenner and we'll call it quits.'

Gemma was disappointed. She wanted to rip off the trolley cover and tell him to help himself. He could buy a new carpet and some new cups and all the biscuits he wanted.

'Ten pounds? Is that all you need? Only we can give you as much as you want.'

'Jimmy...' said Monti, softly.

'A tenner!' he insisted. 'That'll be lovely. That'll buy me another couple of dahlias to fill the corner of that other bed. I've got my eye on some purple ones down the market.'

He felt in his pocket and gave her two five-pound notes in exchange for the twenty she was waving at him. He snapped the note crisply and put it away.

'Thank you, darling,' he said. 'There was no need. Changing the subject, have you seen your flat lately?'

'No,' said Gemma. 'This is the first time I've been back since I ran away.'

He rolled his eyes. 'I say, you'll never believe what they've done to it. That Kasheffi – he's a right basket, he is. He's only gone and turned it into a hotel.'

'Isn't it flats anymore?'

'No, mate. He's knocked it right through. It'll be bed and breakfast, I suppose. For the homeless.'

Gemma thought it strange that Mr Kasheffi was doing something to put a roof over people's heads, given that he was the one who made them homeless in the first place.

'He's only doing it for the *wonga*!' said Ted, pulling a

face and rubbing his fingers together, as if he was counting out notes. 'He's doing it for the money! The council give him hundreds a week for every person he takes in, so you can imagine how many of the poor sods he'll try and cram in!'

Monti was listening to this tirade of anger with great interest. Ted hadn't finished.

'I tell you what really gets me,' he said. 'He's got a dog chained up round the back. Reckons it's his guard dog. Well, I don't think he treats it properly.'

He turned his mouth down in a sad U-shape. 'It's all skin and bone. I creep round the back sometimes and give it a bit of whatever I've had for dinner. I reported it but nothing's been done.'

He looked at Monti and shook his head.

'Breaks your heart, doesn't it? You want to see the weeds and rubbish! Shockin'.'

Gemma looked at him over her teacup. 'What sort of dog was it?'

'A mixture,' he said. 'A big mongrel type. Rusty colour. Come to think of it, it was a bit like the one you had. Still got him, have you?'

Chapter 17

'Do you really think it could be Duke chained up, Monti?'

Monti limped along the pavement trying to keep up with Gemma. Luckily, the trolley acted as a very good walking frame.

'It's not impossible,' she replied. 'There can't be many dogs that look like him and it would be natural enough for a dog to go back to his old haunt.'

A lorry thundered past and Monti recoiled as if she was being charged by a bull rhino. 'This is awful!' she said. 'I'm amazed there's anyone left alive on these streets.'

She'd been nervous crossing the main road on the way to Ted's earlier. Gemma wasn't used to seeing Monti frightened. It made her look like a vulnerable old lady instead of the warrior queen she'd been on her own territory. Gemma had reached out and held her hand.

'You don't have to hold my hand, you're not a baby,' Monti had snapped.

'I feel safer,' Gemma had lied; both of them were well aware who was really doing the looking after.

Gemma pointed in disbelief at the place where her old flat used to be.

'That,' she said, 'was my home.'

There were still bags of sand and bricks lying around on the drive, but the front of the hotel was complete. There was a plaque stuck in the newly turfed grass. It said, 'Spring Park Lodge'.

By the main entrance, there was a panel, numbered 1–8, each with its own illuminated pushbell. The three flats had been converted into eight rooms.

'They must be really small,' said Gemma. 'It must be so cramped.'

The side of the building was as scruffy as it had ever been, with thistles growing up through the broken path. The bins were still there. Just three of them, with the numbers one, two and three painted on carelessly with thick, white paint.

'This is where I used to feed Wolfie, and Mr Ping,' whispered Gemma.

She daren't talk out loud in case Mr Kasheffi was nearby. For all she knew, there could be workmen in the back garden still. There were bootprints, but it was hard to tell how fresh they were.

Using her tracking walk, she edged herself into the garden. There was no one there. She beckoned to Monti, but she wouldn't follow. She wanted to keep guard at the rear.

Apart from a few metres near the house that had been cleared, the garden was strewn with builder's rubbish and rotting wooden pallets. It was completely overgrown and seemed to be reverting back to primeval forest.

The garden shed where she had worked into the night was no longer visible and there was no sign of a dog as far as she could see.

There was a dense arch of brambles growing from the edge of the right-hand wall to the middle of what used to be the lawn. She had to go down on her hands and knees to crawl through this, as the other side was blocked by a pile of old window frames, jagged with broken glass.

Closing her eyes to avoid them being scratched by the thorns, she suddenly struck her head on something wooden.

'Ow!'

At first, she thought it was an old crate of some sort, but as she pulled back the weeds, she realised it was Duchess's kennel. She couldn't believe it was still here. She ran her hand over the roof and noticed that it was still immaculate.

She became aware of the sound of heavy breathing and automatically pressed herself down against the cold earth. Someone must have followed her.

At first, she thought the sound was coming from behind. She held her breath, her mind racing. After a few seconds, she relaxed. It couldn't be a man, he couldn't have crept up on her without cracking a twig or rustling the brambles. She'd have heard him.

No, the noise was coming from in front now. It was rhythmical. It was coming from inside the kennel. She scrabbled round to the front, and there, with his head on his paws, his eyes closed and his fur matted and filthy was the dog Ted has told her about.

'D . . . Duke?'

Crouching down, she placed a trembling hand on his brow and moved it lightly across his head. She could feel his skull. There was a choke chain round his neck. It had rubbed off a strip of fur right down to the skin and caused a band of weeping sores.

'Duke . . . ?'

His eyes opened slowly in their bony sockets. At first, he didn't seem to notice her. Then his nose quivered.

She could hear his tail start to thump inside the kennel as if it was the only bit left of him that had the strength to move. He beat it harder and harder, drumming a tattoo against the kennel floor. Thump, thump, thump!

He raised himself up on his spindly front legs and started to blether and whimper with excitement. Gemma supported him around the waist as he scrabbled with his back legs to get closer to her, pushing his nose under her hair to smell her ears, her neck, her face.

'Ssh, now, ssh!'

But he started to rumble and grunt, she could feel a series of barks building up through his ribs and chest which he wasn't going to be able to stifle.

Somewhere not so far away, a vixen called. Duke clamped his mouth shut, mid-bark. It was the poacher's whistle. Monti was trying to warn her, but it was too late. Gemma felt quickly for the end of the choke chain and unclipped it from the thick, metal ring which was concreted into the ground.

Heavy, muffled footsteps. Expensive shoes covered with plastic bags stamping through the brambles.

'Put that dog back or I'll shoot it.'

Gemma heard the click as Kasheffi pulled back the trigger with his gloved finger. She pulled Duke closer to her. He would have to shoot them both.

'Put the dog back now and get off my property.'

'No!'

He closed one eye and peered down the gun sight, pointing it first at Duke, then at Gemma. He had no qualms about killing either of them. Just as he'd decided which one to shoot first, his concentration was broken by the rattling of plastic wheels behind him.

'How much do you want?' barked Monti.

She jabbed Mr Kasheffi in the back with her whistle. He spun round.

'I said, how much do you want for the dog?'

Mr Kasheffi lowered his gun and looked the old woman up and down as if she disgusted him. He felt for his silk handkerchief and held it over his face in case she carried the plague.

'Oh, but he's invaluable,' said Mr Kasheffi sarcastically. 'A fine dog like this? He's worth his weight in gold, wouldn't you say?'

'Yes, I would.'

With that, Monti ripped the cover off her trolley and began to pelt him with spinning sovereigns, bangles, baubles, rings and plates that struck him around his head, body and knees, making him lift his legs in an idiotic dance. His gun clattered onto some bricks.

'Run, Gemma!'

Monti kicked the gun away with her good foot, drove the petrified man towards the pile of window frames with her trolley and rammed him hard in the back of his knees. Mr Kasheffi smashed face down into a sea of razor-edged glass.

Monti reached into her pocket for the mobile phone and called Mr Spoke.

Linden Spoke threw his head back and laughed so hard, he started choking on the sausage he'd just cooked. Monti had to thump him between the shoulder blades to dislodge the meat from his windpipe. It shot out like a bullet into the clearing where Duke caught it neatly in his jaws and swallowed it.

Monti watched the green tinge fade from Linden's face.

'All right now, Mr Spoke?'

He nodded gratefully.

'I still can't believe you threw all your riches at Kasheffi!' he said.

'I didn't throw them away,' she corrected him. 'I bought a dog for my granddaughter.'

Gemma broke her own sausage in half, blew on it and tossed it to Duke. He gulped it down without chewing and waited for more.

It hadn't taken long to nurse Duke back to health. The day they'd rescued him, Monti had dosed him up, bathed him and rubbed antiseptic into his wounds. Gemma had fed him morsels of rabbit, wrapped him in a sheepskin rug and taken him to bed with her.

When she woke up, he wasn't there. Anxious, after having been without him for so long, she ran into the clearing, calling his name.

She needn't have worried. He was quite safe, sheltering under Cecil B, who seemed very pleased to have the space beneath him occupied again.

'Duke likes your cooking, Linden,' said Gemma. 'Stick another sausage on. I'm starving.'

'Me too,' said Alicia, kicking off her shoes. 'Honestly, Linden. I wish Aunty Amy could see you now.'

'Don't you dare tell Mum!' he whimpered. 'If she knows I've been playing with fire . . . '

But he was only joking. Linden had learnt to do jokes now and found himself relaxed in the company of women. He stabbed a sausage and handed it to his cousin. She looked so much happier, sitting there in her old jeans and jumper with her hair loose and soft.

'Nervous about the trial, Liss?' he asked.

She stretched her arms behind her head and leant back against a tree.

'Yes and no,' she said. 'I'm not sure what Kasheffi's barrister is going to pull out of the bag, but I've got everything I need to send him down for years, hopefully. How did you find out he wasn't even meant to be in the country?'

Linden tapped his nose mysteriously. 'I'm a master detective, aren't I?' he said. 'How's Jim bearing up?'

Alicia blushed slightly. Last night, in his cell, after she had run through the trial procedure with him, she'd stayed and talked way beyond the call of duty. Freeing Jim was no longer a job that had to be done. It had become a labour of love.

'He's okay,' she said. 'He sends you all his best wishes and hopes to see you soon.'

She directed this at Monti, who avoided her eyes.

'Monti, I *wish* you'd go and see him.'

Monti didn't answer. Alicia hugged herself and pleaded. 'But he wants to see you! I know he does.'

Monti stood up stiffly. 'I'm going for a walk,' she said. 'Coming, Jimmy Scar?'

Gemma stood up. She was surprised at being summoned, but followed anyway, leaving Alicia and Linden to wonder what was going on in Monti's mind.

'She's not going to be able to cope like she used to,' Linden confided. 'Not on her own. That limp's getting worse.'

'She could never go into a home, Spooky. It would kill her.'

Linden thought about it.

'I think she's probably immortal. And Liss . . . ?'

'What?'

'Don't ever. . . *ever* call me Spooky, okay?'

'What's wrong, Monti?'

Monti was sitting sidesaddle on a log, staring into space. Gemma sat on the other end, with her back to her. There was a deep sigh, then: 'Jimmy, if you could bring your mother back from the dead, would you?'

It was a difficult question. She wanted to say 'yes' without hesitation, but was it really the truth? It wasn't as if she missed her mother as a person. She couldn't remember anything about her. She just knew that the gap a mother left was a void that needed filling, no matter how good or bad the mother was.

You couldn't replace a mother with a father, because that was like replacing a hand with a foot. Maybe you could learn to walk on your hands or hold things in your feet, but no matter how dexterous you became, you would still be conscious of the difference.

'I'm not sure,' she answered.

'Me neither,' said Monti.

For years, Jim thought his mother had died when he was a baby. He would have formed a glorified picture of her, as humans tend to do with their dead. She was afraid he would be disappointed by the real-life version. When he found out she was not the mother of his dreams, might he not end up hating her? Blaming her? Just as Jimmy Scar blamed her own mother for Not Being There?

'But I only said that because I was angry,' said

Gemma. 'I don't blame her really. It wasn't her fault she wasn't there for me.'

'What's my excuse?' said Monti.

At least Gemma's mother had an excuse. She had been removed prematurely and violently from this earth and with all the will in the world, could not have returned to her daughter in the flesh. She was innocent.

But Monti could have been there for James. She could have tracked him down. It wouldn't have been so very hard. She'd found Gemma, she could have found Will and James. She hung her head in shame.

'I've done it all wrong, Jimmy.'

Gemma turned round to face her. 'But Monti, if you'd married Will, do you really think he'd have been happy playing Dukes and Duchesses in your father's mansion? Think of Ted's dahlias. They were all the gold he needed, you said!'

'But what about James?' insisted Monti. 'He's had to suffer so much. You said so yourself. When I think of you and him in that pokey little flat!'

'I *liked* it!' said Gemma. 'It had wedding cake ceilings and tiles with lilies on all around the fireplace. And, do you know, I think Dad liked it too really? He only complained because he thought I should have something better, just like Will and... and... just like your father!'

Monti tipped her head back so the tears woudn't fall.

'Should I go and see him? You know him so well. Should I go?'

Gemma thought about it carefully. The trial was tomorrow. Jim would need to be calm. He might be angry, he might blame Monti, but it wasn't likely. He came from a long line of men who blamed themselves. He would probably go very quiet and be unable to express himself and Monti would take that the wrong way.

'No. Let him come to you,' said Gemma.

Gemma didn't want her father to meet Monti in prison. First impressions stuck. Against the miserable backdrop of a cell, he might mistake her for a pathetic, dotty old Duchess with a limp.

She wanted him to know who his mother really was. Beyond titles, beyond wealth, beyond family. Because then he would forgive her, if there was any forgiving to be done.

But to know who Monti really was, there was only one meeting place. And that was in the forest.

Gemma spent the next day marking out the foundations. They'd found a perfect spot and loaded Cecil B up with so much equipment, he'd clattered along like an old builder's van.

The riding school horse had been roped in to share the load and Duke, eager to be included, carried the bucket.

Gemma consulted the plans she'd drawn.

'Monti, put a peg in and take the line out further!' she yelled. 'We need to make it big enough for all of us!'

They refused to discuss the trial on purpose. Neither dared to believe Jim might not come home. They set about building the house in the hope that if the gods were watching, they wouldn't be cruel enough to let them break their backs for nothing.

Gemma glanced at her watch discreetly. Why hadn't Linden phoned? He'd promised to let them know how it was going.

'What time is it?' asked Monti.

'Oh, it's early yet!' Gemma lied cheerfully.

It had been decided that Monti would move in with Gemma and Jim once the house was built.

'I can look after myself, you know, in case you hadn't noticed,' Monti had snapped.

'Yes, but I can't,' Linden added.

Linden was desperate to leave his mother and pleaded to be given a room in the new house in return for various duties.

'Such as chopping wood and mending trollies,' he'd said.

He had thrown away his inhaler, and although he still wasn't keen on spiders, he found that here in the forest, he was making up for his lost boyhood. By doing so, he believed he would eventually become the man he wanted to be.

Monti had mumbled about the place getting over-crowded before it was even built.

'I want my own wing!' she insisted. 'I've been on my own for all these years and much as I like a bit of company *occasionally*,' and she stressed the word, 'I have no desire to live in a commune.'

'I'll build you a granny annexe,' said Gemma and got a swift clip round the head.

She'd been wondering what to do about school. She should be going to secondary school next year, but she couldn't face it.

She'd spoken to Alicia, who said legally she didn't have to go to school as long as it could be proved she was receiving a decent education.

'I could teach you,' she said. 'And I'm sure Linden

could help you with your maths.'

'Yes, but not your French,' Linden told her. 'My French is blimmin' awful. I tried to ask where the nearest toilet was when I was in Paris and they sent me to a swimming pool.'

When Gemma told Monti about Alicia's offer, she screwed up one eye and said she wouldn't be at all surprised if Alicia had an ulterior motive for sticking around.

'What's an ulterior motive?'

'Another reason for doing something. She's taken a shine to your father,' she said. 'I can see it in her eyes.'

'See what?'

'Your father's reflection.'

Gemma leant on her spade. She couldn't imagine anyone falling in love with someone as ancient as her dad. She checked her watch again. Oh, please ring, Linden! The trial should have finished ages ago. She tried to make light conversation.

'Were you serious about Alicia falling for Dad, Monti? All that stuff about seeing his reflection in her eyes! You don't even know what he looks like.'

Monti grinned. 'Watch this space,' she said.

Limping along merrily, she scored a square the size of a double bedroom into the soft earth and drew a big heart in the middle.

She remembered Will carving something similar on a tree that grew near her father's mansion. He had cut their initials into the bark: 'M and W'. She'd traced the letters with her finger and noticed that they were mirror images of each other. Or exact opposites, depending on your point of view. They'd swopped rings. She'd given him her gold one with a diamond on, but his hands were so broad, she had to put it on his little finger.

That was a whole generation ago. The tree would have grown gnarled and old, but the heart would still be there, like a little scar.

'Gemma!' called a voice. '. . . Mum?'

Monti dropped the stick.

Jim let go of Alicia's hand and ran towards his mother, arms outstretched, as if he'd just survived his first day at school.